GABBY'S TALES

Allen Border

Copyright © 2017 Allen Border

All rights reserved. No part(s) of this book may be reproduced, distributed or transmitted in any form, or by any means, or stored in a database or retrieval systems without prior expressed written permission of the author of this book.

ISBN: 978-1-5356-0952-4

We consider Allen to be our Spiritual Father. He walks daily with the Lord and is always encouraging others to do the same. He is constantly offering words of wisdom and encouragement. We treasure the time that we spend with him.

— Jenna and Eric Salmon

Allen has a generous and compassionate spirit; he is a loyal and positive individual. These qualities made him a valuable asset to our team.

— John

Hello, my name is Whitney Eckenrode and I was a student of Mr. Allen for many years when I was younger. He has made an impact on my life and many others.

— Whitney Eckenrode

Just a personal note regarding Allen Border. I have known Allen since 2006 when we worked together for DPI specialty foods company. Whenever I worked with him or around him I always found him to be a very conscientious and courteous gentleman. He always put the customers' needs above the company needs which showed a caring nature and concern for his customers. This was not just his work attitude but his personality. He would go out of his way to help anyone that needed his help. He is also a very religious gentleman. It has been an honor to know him for this many years. We don't see each other that often, but when we do it is like no time has passed since our last meeting.

— Keith Burian
Accountant

Introduction

Hello, everyone!

This is A.E. talking. I hope that what you are about to read will inspire you and whoever is reading with you. Some of the story is true. These stories represent my desire to love everyone who crosses my path. May you be blessed as you are reading. And please remember that no matter what happens in your life, you matter!

Contents

Introduction iv
The Birth 1
The Babysitting 11
Crawling and Walking, Oh No! 25
Crazy Christmas 37
Firsts 49
Baby Ethan 61
Kindergarten 73
The Uncle Next Door 89
Faith Without Sight 99
What A Way To Go 113
The Rabbit 127

The Birth

It all began the morning of May 10, 1994. The Boral family was expecting their first baby. Three months ago, the ultrasound had shown it was a healthy girl, but just a week before the due date, the doctors were concerned that it would be a breech birth. Christine, the mother-to-be, was so little and had a weak abdomen from having had two hernias earlier in life. The doctors were sure Christine would have to have a C-section. At two thirty that morning, Christine felt a severe pain and her troubles began.

"Honey, something isn't right," she said while nudging her husband awake.

"Should I get the car, or do you need an ambulance?" her husband Bob asked, picking up the hint of worry in her voice.

"Yes, please call an ambulance. If anything goes wrong, I don't want you to worry," Christine answered as her breathing deepened.

Bob nodded and dialed 911. No sooner had he hung up the phone than he heard a thud. He turned around to find his wife on the floor, unconscious. Moments later, the ambulance arrived and Christine was immediately put on oxygen. Bob then called the church to request prayers through their prayer chain.

"Faith Outreach Center, how may I help you?" Pastor Elmer answered on the other end.

"Pastor Elmer, this is brother Bob Boral. We need prayer for my wife. She just passed out on the floor. The ambulance is here to take her to the hospital and she may be having birth complications."

As soon as Bob got off the phone, he sighed. Christine was rushed to the OR and the doctors could tell something was really wrong..

"We've got a baby in real trouble here! Let's perform a C-section immediately!" one doctor announced.

Christine was still unconscious and her vital signs were weak. Upon performing surgery, they found that the baby's umbilical cord was wrapped around her neck, causing her to kick more than usual. This caused Christine to weaken even more.

"Bob, are you okay?"

Bob turned to face Pastor Elmer and his wife, Beth. "I'm terrified! I don't want to lose my wife or my daughter," he said, sniffling.

Beth handed him a box of tissues. "I know how this hurts, Bob, but let it out and trust God."

Pastor Elmer then began to pray. "Dear Father, we come to you in the name of Your son Jesus, asking for Your protection over this family. Keep Christine and the baby safe, and give Bob the peace that he needs in his heart. Thank you that we can cast our cares to you. In Jesus' name we pray. Amen."

"Thank you for being here for me at this time," Bob said as he looked at Beth and Elmer. "I couldn't think of a better time for the encouragement."

At that moment, something else was happening in the OR that nobody could see. Christine had drifted away into another realm. She saw a bright glow around her and heard a voice speaking very clearly and boldly.

"My daughter, have no fear. My peace is over you and all will be well soon. A spiritual battle is taking place in your body because the enemy senses my power and wants to destroy this child. But fear not! I will win this battle, and your daughter will be well despite the doctors announcing that the *baby is in real trouble here*."

Christine looked up and couldn't see a face, but she knew the voice of her master, Jesus. She moved through his presence and opened her eyes, seeing the hospital room. There were nurses rushing out of the room with her baby.

"Doctor," she whispered, "is my baby going to be okay?"

Dr. Dubig couldn't believe she was awake, but nodded yes, saying, "You relax now. We will do what we need to for both of you."

Christine relaxed and closed her eyes again, not mustering the strength to do or say anymore.

In the next room, three others were helping the baby, who was not breathing. As they were rushing around, the baby's eyes suddenly flew open. Her bright blue eyes were full of life. She took a deep breath and finally started to cry. They were all pleased that the child had responded to CPR and seemed to breathe normally. After cleaning her off, they kept track of her vitals in a special baby bed that looked like a small tent.

Christine was still in danger and her vitals were still very weak. Pastor Elmer stood near a door to the waiting room and it flew open with his friend Dr. Garth standing behind it.

"Pastor Elmer, I'm glad you are here. I have some good news for you all," he announced, looking at the others. "The baby girl is doing fine now and you all will be able to see her soon."

Bob sighed in relief, and then asked, "What about my wife?"

"I'm afraid you'll have to wait a bit longer to see her, sir. We're having trouble keeping her vitals up."

"Will she be okay? Please don't lie to me," Bob said in a somber tone.

"Your wife opened her eyes for a few seconds just after the surgery. We're monitoring her closely and the next several hours will be crucial," he answered honestly.

"How about a name for the little girl, Bob?" Pastor Elmer asked, trying to change the subject.

"I won't do that without my wife's approval. We had several names chosen, but right now none of them seem right to give to her."

"This is an alarming time and I agree that he should wait. Besides, Christine will be okay and she'll be a part of naming the child," Beth said with a motherly smile.

They headed to the nursery and found seven other babies in hospital cribs.

"Whose baby are you looking for?" a nurse asked.

"For my baby girl. I'm Mr. Boral and my wife is Christine. Which baby is ours?"

"Mr. Boral. It's a pleasure to meet you. Your baby is the talk of the whole floor! By the laws of nature, she shouldn't be alive. At birth, the umbilical cord was wrapped around her neck and she stopped breathing.

She was already losing color. Then without warning, her eyes flashed open and she was crying and breathing!"

"Could you tell me what happened to my wife that she had so much trouble?"

"It's hard to explain, sir, but due to the baby being wrapped by the cord, she was kicking, which caused a puncture inside your wife's body. This weakened her body even more and she has some internal bleeding. She will need more time to heal."

"Oh my!" Bob yelped. "Are they both going to be okay?"

"We believe both will be fine, but time will tell. Be patient and hope for the best. Our whole ward is pulling for them."

"Well, we are more than pulling for them. We are praying and believing for a miracle," Pastor Elmer added.

They began more prayer and Bob finished with, "Father, nothing is impossible with you. Touch my wife and give her back the health she needs to be a good mother. Please bless our baby girl as well, and give her the strength to be a blessing for you in the time ahead."

Just then a loud crash was heard as another nurse dropped a tray of supplies. She stood in front of the tent with a wild gaze. The newborn baby girl had both hands in the air and a glow on her face. It appeared as though she were looking right at her dad. Glancing up from the prayer, Bob, Elmer, and Beth noticed it, too.

"Hallelujah! Jesus has just shown us a miracle!" Beth exclaimed with bright eyes.

Meanwhile, in the intensive care unit, another event was unfolding. Christine's vital signs had dropped even lower. A medical team rushed in and prepared her for immediate surgery. They knew something was wrong internally. They paged for Mr. Boral to come immediately to the ICU. Bob peered through a viewing window where several doctors had gathered around. One of them came to tell him that they would need to operate to save her life.

"Not my wife, Satan! She's God's property! Leave her alone and don't come back. In Jesus' name," Bob was screaming at the top of his lungs.

"Calm down, Bob," Pastor Elmer said. "We just prayed and God is in control, not Satan."

Seconds became minutes and minutes became hours. Three hours later, a doctor came from the OR with an update. "Which one of you is Bob?" he asked with a long look on his face.

"That would be me, Doctor." Bob lifted his hand. "How's my wife?"

"Well, I have good news and bad news, sir. The good news is that your wife is recovering and she'll be fine. The bad news is, we had to remove all of her reproductive parts to save her life. She won't be able to have any more children, but will be able to live a fairly normal life."

"How soon can I see her, Doc?"

"She will be unresponsive for several hours, but you are welcome to sit at her bedside now."

"Let's go. Can my pastor come too?"

"Of course. Please try to be quiet. She will need plenty of rest."

Bob got to her room and held Christine's hand. Pastor Elmer and Beth said a farewell prayer for Bob, Christine, and the baby, and then headed out. As they were walking down the hall, Deacon Dufuss from the church met them. He told them that he had a vision for the baby and wanted to see Bob. So Pastor Elmer pointed to the intensive care unit. Mr. Dufuss asked for Mr. Boral, and when he came out to the waiting area, he announced, "Bob, I heard about your situation through the prayer chain. While I was praying, I had a vision about your baby."

"Brad, thank you so much for coming. We really need all the prayers we can get. What was the vision about?"

"I saw a little blonde-haired, blue-eyed girl in a tent-like canopy. She suddenly awoke with an angel beside her that said, 'God's little trumpet blower has arrived.' Then I saw the child growing up and being a great soul-winner for Jesus. She was helping all kind of people in need, showing them the Zoë (Life) of God!"

"How awesome!" Bob's eyes widened in excitement. "I believe God will use her mightily and that's why her birth was so rough. There was spiritual warfare taking place." Bob took a deep breath of relief and then exhaled. Just then a nurse approached Bob, telling him that Christine had opened her eyes and was asking for him. He and Brad entered the room and she looked right at them.

"Gabby. Her name will be Gabby. She will be God's mouthpiece and trumpet blower," Christine said with a low voice.

"Honey, I love you, and I agree that our daughter's name will be Gabby." Bob then alerted the staff of their child's name so she could have a tag written on her crib.

"Sir, we can do even better than that," a nurse name Rebecca replied. "They've taken your baby out of the tent as her condition has become more stable. I'll bring her here for you to hold." In a few moments she reentered the room with the baby. Brad then looked at Bob.

"I'll be right back," he said. When he reentered the room, he handed Bob a long black case.

"What's this?"

"Open it and find out." Brad smiled.

Inside were a beautiful, shiny trumpet and a note that read, *"For the little trumpet player. Love, Mr. and Mrs. Brad Dufuss."*

Bob took it out and Gabby's hand reached to touch it, as if to say, "This is mine."

Gabby and Christine remained in the hospital for another three days. When they went home, a party was held in their honor with many friends and relatives. There was a sign that read "Welcome home, our two little girls! We love you, Christine and Gabby!"

A few minor complications occurred over the next few months but there was nothing serious. Due to the miracles several doctors and nurses had witnessed, a few of them came to Faith outreach center and asked Jesus into their hearts. Gabby's missionary work started at her birth! What will happen next?

This chapter is dedicated to all the hard workers who bring babies into this world. Isaiah 9:6. (NIV)

"For unto us a child is given,
To us a son is given,
And the government will be on his shoulders.
And he will be called
Wonderful, counselor, Mighty God,
Everlasting Father, Prince of Peace."

The Babysitting

When Gabby turned six months old, her parents went out for their anniversary and hired a babysitter from their church to watch her. The girl's name was Brooklyn and she was 16-years-old. She was tall and beautiful with long, reddish-blonde hair that was always tied in pigtails. Upon leaving for the night, Bob and Christine left a list of things for Brooklyn to be aware of. She took the list and told them to have a good time.

"Please, Brook, don't leave any doors unlocked, and stay inside unless there is a disaster," Christine said sternly, keeping her brows furrowed. After sharing a few more words with each other, Bob and Christine bid Brooklyn and Gabby farewell.

They headed for their dinner at the Holiday Inn restaurant five miles away. This was their third anniversary and Bob's parents were treating them. The restaurant was famous for their prime rib and seafood combo. Elwood and Beatrice were Bob's parents. They were fairly wealthy due to Elwood investing in the oil business over fifty years ago. Beatrice, an equally successful person, owned her own beauty shop for the past thirty-nine years. She took Christine down to the main lobby of the hotel while the men ordered their meals. In the lobby was a giant fountain with mermaid statues. This water fountain contained twenty different varieties of freshwater fish. It had a huge, ten-foot waterfall and a filtering system to keep it clean.

"Let's get some pictures here before we eat. My goodness, your gown is beautiful, Christine. Where did you get it?"

"Well, Mom, to be honest, I got it at a local boutique for only $129. My shoes are from Eberly's Shoe Shop and my jewelry is all from my mother."

"Yes, dear, have you seen your mother lately?"

"I would rather not talk about her right now. She has pretty much written me off for marrying a religious man. If you know what I mean."

"This is the perfect time for me to tell you about when I first met Woody. He believed Christianity was a hoax. He had some very bad experiences with Christians who made fun of him."

"So he hated Christians?"

"Hated is too harsh. He just didn't trust them. I saw his good heart and fell in love with him despite the fact that he wasn't saved."

"What made him give in to believing in Jesus?"

"Love. He saw my true love and honesty. I never pushed him about his faith. Just showing him the love of God turned him around."

"I wish my mother would change her attitude. She makes fun of our beliefs and even smirks when we talk about believing around her."

"Have faith and bathe her in your prayers as much as possible. After all, God loves her and so must you."

"She is my mother, and a good one. I pray right now for my mother in Jesus' name. I speak for Shawn and I ask You, Father, to change her into a believer and show her Your love through me in Jesus' name. Amen!"

Meanwhile, back at the Boral house, Brook was giving Gabby her bedtime bottle of milk when the doorbell rang. One of the rules was not to answer the door unless she knew who it was. Since it was November, it was already dark outside by six p.m. It was now almost seven and she decided to take a peek out the window anyway. Under the moonlit sky she noticed a white limousine with its lights on. Being a close friend of the family made it easy for her to recognize that the car belonged to Christine's mother

Shawn. She opened the door and there stood Shawn, a tall, well-dressed woman with fancy, long red hair.

"Hello there, Brooklyn. What are you doing here tonight?" Shawn said while stepping inside.

"Hi, Mrs. Matthews. I am babysitting Gabby. The Borals are out for their anniversary dinner with Bob's parents."

"Oh my, is it their anniversary? How foolish of me to forget that. Where is my darling little grandchild?"

"She is in her crib. I was just giving her a bedtime bottle. Come on into her room while I finish feeding her."

"Hi, beautiful. Are you a hungry little girl?" Shawn exclaimed, looking wide eyed at Gabby. "Can I finish feeding her for you, Brooklyn?"

"Sure, here you go," Brooklyn said handing Gabby and the bottle over to her grandmother. Immediately Gabby began to scream.

"It's okay, Gabby. This is your grandma Shawn. She wants to feed you," Brooklyn responded.

Even though Gabby was too little to understand, she really didn't like Shawn to hold her. Brooklyn took her back and the crying immediately stopped. As soon as the feeding was over, Brooklyn rocked Gabby to sleep and placed her in her crib. The crib was a gift from Shawn. It was beautiful. It had a large, rotating music box above it that played "Mary had a Little Lamb" and the sides were made of a new kind of vinyl. After the baby had settled down enough to lie down in her crib, the two ladies went into the sunken living room. They chatted for about an hour until Shawn decided it was time for her to leave. She thanked Brooklyn for the visit and gave her a gift certificate to a local pizza shop for two all-loaded pizzas and a two-liter bottle of soda.

Back at the restaurant, the four adults had finished their wonderful meals and headed for a concert in the hotel's largest room. The special music that night was the performance by a father and daughter whose group was called The King's Pair. They were a Christian contemporary group with a guitarist, keyboardist, and drummer.

"This duo sings some of the best music and it's all written by the father. What do you think of them Bob?" His father was inquiring to find out his likes and dislikes.

"Well, Dad, I love their style. And the daughter reminds me of when Christine sang in church as a teen."

"Oh, yes! She was awesome back then. Do you think she will ever sing a solo again?"

"I hope when Gabby is old enough, the two of them will perform together as a daughter and mother team."

"Oh, Bob, you just have too much pride in your little girl already. Besides, how do we know that she will even like music?" Christine interjected, not seeming too enthusiastic about the idea.

"Christine, why did you stop singing at the age of seventeen? You had so much potential, and I say, a gifted voice." Beatrice seemed to be egging her on again.

"My beloved mother told me to be more concerned with my grades than with singing religious music. I obeyed and even turned down an offer to sing a solo at the Holy Ghost convention just before Amy Grant was to perform that year."

"Your mother didn't know how gifted you were. And I believe her distaste for God is her biggest problem. I believe God is going to change all of that soon," Elwood chimed in, knowing how God had changed him.

"If God can change my mother, He can change anybody. Sometimes I think she is worse than Paul was before his conversion."

"Well, that's just my point. God got Saul's attention, and He will do the same for your mother." Elwood smiled, and then looked at the group on stage as they were preparing for their closing number.

Shawn got into her car and thought about how unhappy Gabby was in her arms. Her mind then flashed back to when she had given birth to Christine, who did the very same thing. Christine's father could calm his daughter down as easily as Brooklyn could calm Gabby. Before she could bring her attention back to reality, Shawn's car was sliding off the road. After flipping upside down, it skidded to a stop in a nearby ditch just off the road. She wasn't badly hurt, but the door was jammed and she needed to get out of the car. Within minutes, help arrived. An old man, all dressed up, came over and broke the window to get Shawn to safety.

"Are you okay, lady?" he asked in a gentle voice. "Do you need an ambulance?"

"I don't think so. I'm just a little bit dizzy. Thank you for helping me, sir. What's your name?"

"I am Mr. Lox from up the street. I was just on my way home from a revival meeting at our church when I saw your car in the ditch."

"That figures," Shawn added with a touch of disgust in her voice.

"What do you mean by that?" Mr. Lox asked as he heard approaching sirens coming down the street.

"Oh, it's not important. It just seems that every time I'm in trouble, only Christians come to my rescue."

"Well, that's because Jesus loves you. Do you know Him as your personal savior?"

At that very moment, Brooklyn went into Gabby's room and started to pray for Shawn. She didn't know about the accident yet, but felt led to pray for her. She looked in the crib and noticed Gabby was staring right at her with a large smile in her face, like she was agreeing with the prayer.

"You say Jesus loves me. What kind of God allows people to wreck their cars?" Shawn responded in a frustrated tone of disgust.

"Well, my dear lady, it's not that He allows it. It is usually our fault somehow. Do you remember what happened just before you wrecked?"

"Yes, but that's none of your business. However, you're right. I had my mind on something else and wasn't watching what I was doing."

"You see, it was your fault, lady. But God protected you and you came out of the car unharmed. That is what we call a miracle. So you see, He does love you."

Shawn thought about this for a few moments and then asked, "How do you get to know this savior Jesus?"

"Just like asking someone for a favor. You ask him to forgive your sins and come into your heart. It's that simple. Are you ready to do it?"

"I think so. Can He fill the empty feelings I have sometimes?"

"Yes, He will, and you will have victory through Him when those feelings try to come back. Just repeat after me and you'll get there."

"Okay. Wait! Can I tell Him in my own special way?"

"Sure. I'm just here to guide you through it."

"Dear God or Jesus, please forgive my feelings about you for all these years. I have hurt you and myself deeply. I give my life to you now and repent of all my faults, or I guess you call them sins. Thank you for Your forgiveness, and cleanse me now in Your name. Amen. Wow, that was easier than I thought."

"Now you just have to trust Him. You stay here. I'll help the fireman at your car."

"Oh, my car! I almost forgot. Will it be okay?"

Just then a fireman approached her and asked, "Are you okay, lady?"

"Yes, but what about my car? Will I be able to drive it again?"

"Well, lady, I'm afraid not. Your gas tank busted and the windshield is broken, and to be honest, you're lucky to be alive. I'm shocked that your car didn't catch on fire. It is a miracle."

"Yes, my first one in my new life."

"I beg your pardon? What do you mean?"

"Oh, I was just making an observation out loud"

"Are you sure you don't need medical treatment, ma'am?"

"Yes, I'm sure. By the way, where did the older man go that was here. I wanted to thank him again"

"What older man? When we got here, you were all alone and unconscious. We still don't know how you got out of the car without a scratch."

"You had to see him. He said he was Mr. Lox."

"Oh, I get it. When we first found you, you were unconscious, but then you started coming back around and you kept saying, 'The locks, the locks. I just need to open the locks!' You see, all your doors were locked and you were outside the car. I think you bumped your head and got a little confused."

Meanwhile, the Boral family had just finished the concert and was getting ready to leave. A police car was just pulling into the space next to Bob and Christine's vehicle and two officers got out. One officer looked over and recognized Christine. "Hey, Christine. It's Joe Fortina from high school. Are you okay?"

"Hi, Joe. I'm fine. Why do you ask so solemnly?"

"You didn't hear yet? Your mother just crashed her car about a mile from your house. What a mess. I still can't believe she got out of there unscathed."

"Where is she now?"

"I believe the fireman in charge was taking her to a local hotel. Her car was totaled. And get this. She was found outside the car and all the doors were locked. Weird!"

"No, Joe, that is Jesus Christ. We prayed for her tonight and God gave her a miracle." She turned to her husband and said, "Bob, take me to the Hilton, please. I'm sure that's where they took her. Thanks, Joe, for the information."

"Best of luck to you all. And tell your mom she's in our prayers."

Bob's parents said their farewells and went home. The whole way home they talked about the great miracle that God had done for Shawn, and what a great time they had at dinner.

Christine and Bob got to the Hilton and asked for Shawn's room. The clerk asked who they were, and then called the room to see if it was okay for them to go up. Of the eight floors of the hotel, Shawn was on the seventh in room 777.

Shawn opened the door and grabbed Christine saying, "Have I got a story for you! Please come and sit down." She told them the whole story and they all praised God together.

After leaving the hotel, Christine called home to check in and tell Brooklyn they were on their way home. Brooklyn finished the call by adding, "When you get here, I have a story to tell you."

"We have one to tell you, too. We'll see you in about ten minutes."

Upon arrival, the Borals met Brooklyn at the front door. She helped them inside and told them about Shawn's visit. "Mrs. Boral, every time Shawn touched or even looked at Gabby, Gabby cried. It's like Gabby didn't like her spirit or something"

"I know, dear. My mother never was good with children. However, I believe that will soon change."

"Why do you say that?"

"Right after she left you, she got into a bad car wreck"

"Oh, my goodness. Will she be all right? You know, I felt led to pray for her right after she left."

"Thank you. Your prayers, plus ours at dinner, did a miracle. She got out of the wreck safely, had an encounter with God, and got saved."

"Hallelujah! Babysitting led to a salvation. That's awesome!"

"Amen! Now here is your payment, and Bob will take you home so it's not past your curfew. Give your parents a thank you from us for letting you come."

"I will. One more thing, give Gabby a kiss for me in the morning and tell her that I love her."

"No problem. We will call you again when we need a babysitter." Brooklyn and Bob left while Christine checked on Gabby.

The next morning, while feeding Gabby at the table, Bob and Christine discussed the events of the night before. When they brought up Shawn's conversion, Gabby lifted her hands above her head like a gesture of praise and laughed.

What could possibly be next in this child's life of excitement? This is A.E. inviting you to enjoy the next chapter of Gabby's life. Until then, I leave you with a verse to think about: Acts 16:31. Thank you!

Acts 16:31 (ESV) And they said, "Believe in the lord Jesus and you will be saved, you and your household."

This chapter is dedicated to all the selfless mothers out there looking to give the best to their children.

Crawling and Walking, Oh No!

BY THE AGE OF ONE Gabby began crawling and getting into everything imaginable. Low cupboard doors were an Indiana Jones adventure. She soon earned the title of "one girl crawling disaster unit."

One morning Christine was doing laundry and a basket of clothing looked like a mountain of fun for Gabby. So she grabbed one side of the container and dumped it all over.

"Gabby! You are a little troublemaker. I just folded all those clothes," her mom cried out.

In a moment, from under the pile of clothing, appeared a face, and a laugh came out that sounded like a hyena with laryngitis.

"I can't turn my back on you for a minute. Nonetheless, this is a Kodak moment." Christine quickly grabbed her camera from the shelf and snapped a photo of this basket-cased child.

Every day was a challenge. They started to padlock the drawers and cupboards, but they weren't fast enough. Gabby had already turned the whole house into a walking disaster area. One Friday evening Christine had some errands to run, giving Bob the pleasure of watching the female version of Dennis the Menace.

Gabby was on the living room floor that was covered with a thick brown carpet. Bob was sitting in his recliner reading the daily news. He didn't notice that Gabby had already created a disaster. Gabby was looking at the recliner and saw a small opening under her dad. *A hiding place,* she thought. Bob had momentarily dozed off when he suddenly heard a weird noise. He got up to close the recliner, not even noticing that Gabby was underneath the chair. When he realized she wasn't in sight, he began looking for her throughout the house. Even though Gabby was in a tight spot, she kept quiet, thinking it was like hide-and-seek. This lasted for ten minutes and Bob started to panic. Calling out her name a few times and hearing nothing, he walked to another part of the house. Suddenly, Gabby realized she was alone and wanted out. She began to cry, and when Bob heard her whimpers, he followed them right to the chair.

"How did you get in there?"

She couldn't talk, but grabbed her dad's hand and stood for the first time. Bob was so concerned about her that he didn't even notice that she was standing. Then it hit him, and he immediately grabbed for his cell to call Christine. However, it wasn't where he'd remembered putting it. Then he heard it ring. It was inside the recliner. It must have fallen when he went to sleep. He bent over to pick it up and heard a familiar voice coming from it.

"Is everything all right at home?"

It was Christine. Apparently, Gabby had pushed speed dial while in her hiding place. Bob picked it up and said, "All right? Your little angel crawled under my recliner and was playing with my cell phone. Guess what?"

"She called me, heard my voice, and got quiet."

"You're no fun. That's probably exactly what happened. And a few moments later she stood up!"

"She did? Oh NO!!! Now nothing in the house is safe. If she starts walking, the steps might become a war zone."

"Oh, dear, quit panicking. God will use his angels to help us."

"I know, but I'll still need eyes in the back of my head. I'm getting in the car now. I'll be home in five minutes."

"Okay, it'll keep her out of mischief until then."

It only took Gabby three days until she was a walking time bomb waiting to explode.

The following Wednesday morning was the women's Bible meeting at the Boral's. The usual attendance was around four people, but today eight women came. Gabby didn't waste any time showing off her walking and running skills. She greeted each lady. The first to arrive was Mrs. Hernandez, a fine lady with six children. Her youngest was two years old, a girl named Alison who was in the terrible twos stage. Just what Gabby needed, a second instigator! After all eight women had arrived, the girls were placed in a playpen. They were fine until Alison got selfish over an orange toy block. Gabby tried to take it from her but Alison promptly tossed it out of the playpen into the middle of the adult circle. Mrs. Myers put it back only to watch her toss it again and hit her in the rear end! Everyone laughed and Gabby began to scream. She was so loud that she awoke a sleeping baby in the other room. The Bible study became a chorus of cries and screams from the children. It took thirty minutes to calm things down.

Mrs. Belch was the leader and decided it was time to pray over the children. Mrs. Whitecomb's newborn was already back to sleep so they prayed over him first. His name was Aaron. Next was Billy, a four-year-old with a jolly spirit. He giggled all the way through the prayer. Alison followed. Her mom held her while they all prayed. She squirmed like a worm, but made it through despite having a dirty diaper by the end of the prayer. It was her way of saying amen. Gabby was last. During the prayer, she was still, but at the end of it she added her amen by vomiting on the carpet.

"I'm so embarrassed! Let me clean up this mess so we can finish our meeting," Christine said, looking very upset.

"Christine, it's okay. We all had these moments. We can leave now and give you time with your little one," Mrs. Belch said with a large smile.

Just then, a crash was heard in the kitchen. They all rushed in and saw Jumper the dog add his two cents to the day by knocking over the trash can.

"This is becoming a three-ringed circus! I don't know what to say." Christine was becoming very nervous.

"Mrs. Boral," a voice said from the other end of the kitchen.

"What now?"

"Your daughter just left you a Kodak moment. Come and see." It was Mrs. Williams, the next-door neighbor.

Sure enough, Gabby had opened the only cupboard door that wasn't yet padlocked and was sitting on a frying pan, full of her messy diaper.

"Ladies, I am so embarrassed," Christine said, exasperated. "Please forgive me as I ask you all to leave while I get things back in shape." She was even redder in the face than before.

"Nonsense! We will all help you and then go home. That's what sisters in the Lord do."

It was Mrs. Carlson, who began cleaning up the scattered trash. They all pitched in and then headed home. Due to the situation, Christine decided not to hold the Bible group at her home anymore. As a matter of fact, she was so upset that she quit attending the group altogether. The ladies would all take turns calling her but she kept making up excuses. One Wednesday morning, Bob woke early to go golfing with a client. Before leaving the house, he decided to wake his wife and finally confront the situation.

"I am going golfing today with my number one client. I should be home by four or five. I also got a call from Mr. Carlson asking why you don't attend the women's Bible group anymore."

"Honey, with Gabby getting into everything, I'm concerned about the mess she might make at someone's house. When she grows out of this stage, I will return to the group."

"But you haven't even gone to church for the last few weeks. What's your reason for that?"

"I don't want Gabby to be a burden for the nursery staff. And I won't allow her to disrupt the service, either. I have too much respect for God's house to let that happen."

"Oh yeah, but in the meantime, your own spiritual life takes a step back. You know better. This will change. As your husband, I must look out for you as well as my daughter. We will discuss this more tonight when I get home."

"Worrywart! I will be fine. Besides, I can spend more time training Gabby for her future. Now go tee off before you T me off. Okay?"

"Okay, dear. See you later. May your day be a blessed one with Gabby."

Bob headed to his car. Gabby woke at the sound of the car starting in the garage, which was under her room. The muffler had a small hole so it was a bit louder than usual. At least it was a good alarm clock for Gabby, which warned her that her dad was leaving for the day.

A loud cry came from Gabby's room. Her mother knew what that meant. She was in need of a diaper change and it also meant, I'm hungry! Feed me!

"WAHHHHH!!!!! WAHHHHHH!!!! WAAAHHHHHH!!"

"Just one minute, young lady. I am finishing last night's dishes. I'll be right there."

Christine's voice already carried a tone of disgust. Gabby continued her boisterous sounds until her mother picked her up out of the crib. At the same time the phone rang and so did the doorbell.

"Not again. I think I'll join the circus for some peace and quiet," Christine muttered to herself, and then yelled toward the door. "Hang on there. I'll be down in a moment."

She rushed to the door with a bottle in one hand, a screaming baby in the other, and a cell phone clamped to her ear by her shoulder. At the door stood her mother Shawn. Shawn took one look at her daughter and recognized the distress on her face. She had been there many times herself so she took Gabby in her arms, and Gabby stopped crying. Christine was so frustrated that she didn't even realize Gabby wasn't crying anymore.

"I will take Gabby to her room. Give me the bottle and I'll feed her. You take care of your phone call." Shawn headed to the bedroom singing, "Mary Had a Little Lamb" and feeding Gabby her bottle.

"Hello. This is Christine. How can I help you?" On the other end was Mrs. Fields asking for the donation for the women's auxiliary.

"Mrs. Fields, I will send you my usual donation of fifty dollars next week. Thanks for calling." She hung up and didn't even give Mrs. Fields time to respond. She quickly headed to Gabby's room and found her daughter laughing in Shawn's arms. Gabby was getting tickled and kissed on her belly.

"Thanks, Mom, for helping me out. It's like a—"

"Three-ringed circus, right? You would rather join that now for peace and quiet."

"Yeah. How did you know that?"

"Dear daughter, I was in the same shoes many years ago myself. This morning I felt led by God to come here. And now I know why."

"Really? Wow! I want to hear that story."

"When I was your age, I already had all three of my children. Your father was always at work. And my circus never stopped. I had diapers to change, lunches to prepare, laundry to do, pets to take on walks, and a phone that was like a New York switchboard operator's. Believe me, I understand."

"Is this supposed to make me feel better?"

"Maybe not, but let me tell you that you have one ingredient that I never had then."

"What would that be?"

"Have you forgotten your Jesus? He can give you the peace that you need, and he is no circus. He is real."

"Mom, for the first time I must fully agree with you."

"Good. That's a blessing, but let me tell you more. You only have one child. And she's blessed. She's God's handiwork. And you need to be thankful that he entrusted her to you. That is an honor just like you are an honor to me."

"Do you mean that? I'm an honor to you?"

"When you were little, I didn't have Jesus to give me that peace. But your dad did. He never pushed Jesus on me, but he was always at church and I used to hate him for that."

"You mean Dad did know the Lord?"

"Yes, honey. But he was quiet about his faith. You children were the only ones he would talk to about Jesus. That's why you all got quiet around him, because he gave you peace.

"I don't remember much about Dad, Mom. How old was I when he died? And you never talked about Dad's death."

"You were three years old. Your dad went on a men's retreat for a weekend. He thought it would be an encouragement for his walk of faith. They all took separate cars, and it was a winter weekend we will never forget. February 11, 1973. We had a blizzard. Three feet of snow. Your dad's car hit a snow bank and flipped over. He tried to get out, but the gas tank exploded and he was burned alive."

"Well, how badly was the car burned?"

"Totally, everything but the frame. But let's get back to you being an honor to me. I never said much to you after you married Bob. However, his faith is much like your dad's was, but more outspoken."

"Yeah, he is a bit bold sometimes. But I like him that way."

"You are blessed daughter. But not trusting God now would be a big mistake. Gabby is young and lively, just like you were. As a matter of fact, her actions are a spitting image of yours as a child."

"Oh, she has embarrassed me so badly sometimes. I feel like I don't matter at all anymore."

Just then Gabby let out a burst of gas, sounding like an alarm going off, and she laughed.

"See what I mean, Mom?"

"Oh, that's mild compared to what you did. We were at a ladies meeting in church and you farted out loud, vomited, and then pooped."

"Not me!"

"Oh yes, you! I wanted to hide in the closet. But I just had stuffed it full of the toys you threw all over the floor along with your empty bottle that wet my work papers. I had no time to clean it up."

Then it happened. Gabby grabbed the plastic cross hanging from her crib and pointed it at her mother. "Oh my! Your daughter just gave you a sign. Get back with your Lord before you slip away."

Gabby smiled and put the cross down and nodded her head yes in agreement.

"Gabby, you truly are my little angel. Jesus, forgive me for not trusting you more. I let my pride keep me from being faithful, and expected my daughter to be perfect. You're the only perfect one. Bless my daughter and me to be better with each other and trust you more in our shortcomings."

Gabby fell asleep and Shawn left. That night Christine called all the women from the Bible group asking for their forgiveness. When Bob got home, they had a nice talk. Things became more normal. However, Gabby did continue to have her moments.

Three days later she spilled her bottle on her mother's new evening gown. She also broke a candy dish and left behind the evidence of a dirty diaper in front of the heater vent.

A month later in the nursery at church, she grabbed one of the nursery worker's glasses, tossing them against the wall and breaking them. At the end of all of these events, Gabby had cost her parents over a thousand dollars in damages before she started to settle down. I don't know about you, boys and girls, but this sounds to me like a future of excitement for the Boral household. Your memory verse for this story comes from Philippians 4:32. Many blessings! A.E.

This chapter is dedicated in honor of Antonette Fort who raised six children.

Crazy Christmas

CHRISTMAS AT THE BORAL HOUSE was always a beautiful time. Decorations were in every room and the outside was always a local attraction. Bob would start decorating Halloween week to counteract the evil things around them. The pine tree out front was thirty feet tall this year and it was very time consuming to put the lights on it. It took more than 500 lights to cover the tree and a friend brought over his lift truck to reach the top. Christine would provide dinner for everyone that came from church to help decorate. It took five men and three ladders to finish the tree, and five more volunteers to put the decorations up on the house.

Gabby was just learning to talk. And it was nonstop. A few words were clear, like "mama" and "papa," and her favorite word was "no." While decorating, the other children kept Gabby entertained. They played games like hide-and-seek, and incorporated other things to keep her busy. Gabby found the tree in the living room to be the most engaging object of all. She had decided that it would make a great hiding place during hide-and-seek. However, that was a bad idea. Naomi, the eight-year-old girl next door, was always very hyper. She saw Gabby behind the tree and went to get her, and disaster soon followed. She lost her balance and knocked over the towering tree. The tip that once reached the ceiling was now draped over the sofa where three ladies were sitting. Thankfully, the tree was artificial and the needles didn't stab the ladies. A few scratches occurred, but nobody was seriously hurt. Gabby just laughed, and Naomi ran to another room hoping nobody would know she'd done it.

"Naomi! Get back here now so we can talk." It was her mother Joni whose tone seemed to mean that a spanking was coming.

"Yes, Mother. How's the decorating coming along?" She looked up inquisitively, hoping to avoid hearing about what had just happened with the tree.

"Oh, it was just going fine until the neighborhood lumberjack decided to knock down the tree. Could you tell me how that happened?"

"Well, Gabby was hiding there and I saw her so I went to get her and the tree wasn't big enough for both of us so it decided to fall."

"I somehow feel that a girl named Naomi was just a little careless and knocked over the tree. Therefore, she owes somebody an apology."

"Okay. Mrs. Boral, I'm sorry I knocked your tree over." Naomi lowered her head.

"You're forgiven, Naomi, but I think the ladies it fell on need an apology also."

"Sorry, ladies. I'll be more careful from now on."

"Gabby." Christine turned to her daughter who had finished crawling on the floor. "No going behind the tree again or you'll get spanked." Gabby nodded her little head as if to say she understood.

By the end of the day the decorations inside and out were all up. A feast was served for all at the dinner hour and then everyone left for home.

Christmastime came quickly. All the neighbors' houses were decorated and the whole town was aglow like a galaxy of its own. Christmas week was always busy at the Boral household. Grandma Shawn would come over to bake cookies and wrap presents. This year she brought a new recipe for chocolate chip cookies with M&M's and Reese's Pieces.

"Gabby, you get the first taste. Come and get it!" she announced.

Gabby's eyes lit up like the Christmas tree as she bit into the first cookie. She grabbed Shawn's leg in thanks and Shawn bent over to receive a chocolate mess of a kiss.

"Oh, I guess I got the second taste from that kiss! That must mean your cookie was good. Huh, Gabby?" Gabby then stretched out her hand as if to say please give me another. Just then, a knock on the door was heard and Christine headed over to answer it.

"Happy holidays, everybody!" It was cousin Joyce with her fresh-baked chocolate cake that she brought every year as a gift. It was Bob's favorite. It was covered with peanut butter icing.

"Here's your cake. Why hello, Gabby! You're getting so big."

"Look out!" yelled Shawn. But she was too late. Gabby had managed to reach the sheet of cookies and they tumbled to the floor with a crash.

"What a mess! Gabby, you are just on a role this season. First the tree, and now the cookies. What's next?" Christine seemed rather upset. They quickly got the mess picked up and Shawn baked the second batch.

"Christine, you made a similar mess when you were two years old. Aunt Helen baked her famous cake covered in icing and you put both your hands right on top of it. "

"*I* did *that*? Hmm, it must run in the family. Did I totally ruin it?"

"Not quite, but close. You sure had fun licking off the icing, though."

"Well, Mom, at least I got some enjoyment out of it."

"True. That is, until you got spanked for it. At least Gabby's wasn't quite as messy." They all laughed about it, and Gabby went up to her room to take a nap after being cleaned up.

"Aunt Shawn, what's your favorite Christmas memory of all time?" Joyce asked.

"Oh, that's easy. The time your dad Dale spilled the hot apple cider over the dog Trixie. And his reaction was, 'Just what I wanted for Christmas! A big hotdog!'"

"*My* dad did that?"

"Yes. And then your dad took Trixie out into the snow to cool him off. The dog turned out okay, but your dad never survived the embarrassment."

"Mom, I remember that event!" Christine added, and then turned to Joyce. "We even had fun with Dale that year by giving him an extra five-pack of hotdogs for Christmas. This reminds me of another thing, Mother."

"What's that, Christine?"

"Do you still have that baby boy doll you gave me one year for Christmas?"

"Oh, I just donated that doll to the church for their manger scene this year. Do you still want it?"

"I thought I could pass it on to Gabby this year."

"We should take Gabby to the manger scene and you can tell her about baby Jesus!"

"Great idea! We can go there tomorrow. Will you join us, Joyce?"

"No, thanks. I will be at my sister Barb's house tomorrow to do more baking."

They all sat down and shared a pot of coffee, and then Joyce went home. The next morning after breakfast, Shawn, Christine, and Gabby headed to the church. Outside was a beautiful hand-built manger scene. The figures were all hand-carved from wood except for the baby Jesus. Christine talked to Gabby about the baby Jesus and then let her hold the baby. Gabby smiled wide and said, "Baby Jesus." Shawn and Christine both shed a tear as they placed the baby back in the manger. They went into the church and found Pastor Elmer praying at the altar. He heard them enter and got up.

"Good morning, ladies. I'm so glad you're here. I need a favor."

"What is it, Pastor?" Shawn asked.

"We have a box of food that needs to be delivered to the local homeless shelter. Are you able to take it there today?"

"Of course! Whom do we ask for when we get there?"

"Christine, his name is Frank Miller. He runs the shelter and divides the food equally among many people. He will meet you out front to collect the box. It is very heavy so I will load it for you here and he will unload it there."

"No problem, Pastor. I'll pull the van over by the door now." Christine, Shawn, and Gabby drove to the shelter and were met by a tall, dark-haired man.

"Hello, ladies! I am Frank Miller. Pastor Elmer said that you would be dropping off some goods for us."

"Hi. I'm Christine, and this is Shawn and my daughter Gabby. We have one big box for you in the back. I will open the hatch for you."

"My, this *is* a big box. Thank you. What's inside of it?"

"Pastor Elmer told me it's all food."

"Well, thank you so much. Please come inside to meet some of our volunteers."

Alice was the first person they met. She gave them a tour, and soon they wound up in a large room with about fifty people and lots of beds. Gabby's eyes were immediately drawn to a little girl sitting on a bed by her mother. She ran over to the bed to say hi. Christine and Shawn then began talking to the mother.

"Hello. My name is Christine Boral. This is my mother Shawn and my daughter Gabby. And what's your name, ma'am?"

"My name is Jeanie Martin and this is my four-year-old daughter Esmeralda. We sometimes call her Ezz or Ezzy for short."

"How long have you been in this shelter, Jeanie?" Shawn asked.

"I've only been here three weeks, but I've been homeless for a year."

"How did you become homeless?" Christine asked.

"We lived in a trailer until my husband ran away. I haven't been able to find a job and we could no longer pay the bills."

"Do you have a car?" Christine wondered.

"No, my husband took that so I have no transportation."

"How did you end up at this shelter?" Shawn asked.

"We hitchhiked and a kind lady took us here."

"How far from here did you live?"

"About twenty miles."

"Don't you have any relatives that can help?"

"My family disowned me years ago."

"Well, how about if we pick you up for our church service on Sunday morning?"

"That's a very nice offer but I don't have anything to wear."

"Don't worry about that. We're not fancy at our church. Just come the way you are. My daughter Gabby loves to be with other children. I'm sure they would enjoy each other's company."

"Well, okay. What time should we be ready?"

"We'll pick you up around 9:15."

"Excuse me ladies. Oh, I see you've met Jeanie."

"Yes, and we've invited her to our church on Sunday morning. Is that okay?"

"Sure is. Nobody's tied down here so we'll see you then. Thanks again for the food!"

When Shawn and Christine turned around again, they saw Gabby and Ezzy sitting on the floor playing with Gabby's dress-up doll that she carried with her almost everywhere. When they all left, Ezzy cried and her mom tried to settle her down.

That night, the shelter took a bus group out to see the Christmas lights. They made two stops. One was at the local orchard and the other was at the manger scene. Although there was quite a bit of traffic at the church, Ezzy focused on the manger scene. Since she had played with Gabby's doll earlier in the day, she thought she could play with this one. She picked up the baby Jesus. One of the church leaders walked by and frowned as he said, "Don't touch." She laid it back down and then watched until nobody was looking and quickly tucked it into her coat. Her mother was busy talking to someone and didn't notice what she had done. So they entered the bus and headed to the shelter. When they got back to the shelter, Esmeralda kept the baby doll hidden under the bed.

On Sunday morning, the Borals picked up Jeanie and Ezzy for church. When they got there, Gabby headed straight for the manger scene. She pointed at the empty manger and uttered, "Baby Jesus!" Several people gathered around and realized that baby Jesus was missing. As Jeanie and Ezzy walked by, Ezzy wouldn't look at the manger scene. Ezzy saw that everyone was concerned and she knew it was her fault. She didn't know how to respond. After church was over, the Borals brought Ezzy and Jeanie back to the shelter. When they got inside, Ezzy immediately grabbed Gabby's hand and led her to the bed. Pulling the doll out, she handed it to Gabby.

"Baby Jesus!" Gabby exclaimed.

The adults all turned and saw the doll being placed in Gabby's arms. Jeanie approached her daughter and asked, "Where did you get that?"

"I took it from the manger last night because I wanted the baby Jesus to be warm."

"I see, honey. Well, that's called stealing and we're not supposed to steal. But I'm proud that you're giving it back."

"Jeanie, may we talk a minute?" Christine asked.

"Yeah, what is it?"

"Follow me." The two women headed to the front desk. "Alice."

"Yes, Mrs. Boral?"

"A situation has just arisen that I need your help with."

"Ezzy took the baby Jesus from our manger scene at church last night. She meant no harm. I need your permission to take her and her mother somewhere for a while this evening. Would that be all right?"

"It's okay, but lunch will soon be served and she might miss that."

"That's fine. I'll treat them for lunch. This is important."

"All right, but make sure she's back by 4:30 for our supper hour."

Christine smiled and thanked Alice, and then offered to take Jeanie and Ezzy out to lunch. After lunch was finished, they headed to the Toys "R" Us. Once inside, Christine looked at Jeanie and said, "I want you and Ezzy to pick out a doll and I will buy it for her."

"Why are you doing this?"

"Your daughter needs to show her love. That's why she took the doll." Christine smiled at Esmeralda. "So I'll give her one so that she can show her love. And by the way, Jeanie, the Robertson family in our church has a spare room. They told me this morning they will give it to you. Also, Mr. Robertson will let you work for him."

Jeanie began to cry as she said, "Never in my life has anyone ever showed me such love."

"Jesus loves you and Esmeralda very much. If you follow Him, you'll know what true love is."

From that day forward, Jeanie and Ezzy's life turned around. The friendship between the Borals and the Martins grew stronger day by day. Jeanie became the head receptionist at Mr. Robinson's business and within a year she purchased a brand new trailer.

This chapter is dedicated to all the homeless people in our world today. Will you reach out your hand and help one? This is A.E. encouraging you to read Colossians 3:17-23. Until next time!

Firsts

ALL PARENTS LOOK FORWARD TO many firsts in their child's life. Some of these are fun. For example, a child's first tooth, their first word, the first time they crawl, and their very first steps. The list goes on. Other firsts, however, can be rather ugly. The first stinky diaper, their first boo-boo, the first time they get sick, or their first major injury.

Gabby was pretty average with her first tooth at three months and crawling at five months. She also surprised her parents with a very special moment when she spoke her first word—"no." However, in this story we are going to share her first disaster involving fear.

Gabby was just shy of a year old when an attempt to sleep led to a disaster. Christine tucked her into her crib and turned the lights off before crawling into her own bed. It was May, just before Gabby's birthday. The weather that night was warmer than usual and they had to turn on the fan to keep her cool. The fan was about five feet from Gabby's crib, but faced away from her because the family didn't want to risk her catching a cold. Their pet dog Jumper slept in the room also. He was a Boston terrier mixed with poodle. Around 2:00 a.m., Bob was woken up by the sound of a crash.

"Christine, wake up! Something just fell or broke. You check on Gabby and I'll look around." Just then Bob realized the other side of the bed was empty. Christine had heard the same noise and had already left the room to rush to Gabby.

"What have I done to you, Gabby?" Christine asked, tears welling up in her eyes.

"What's wrong, honey?" Bob said as he rushed toward the crib.

"She's on the floor, under the fan, and she is bleeding. CALL 911 NOW!"

"Will do. I'll get some ice and a towel, too. What in the world happened?"

Christine couldn't respond. She turned off the fan immediately and tossed it aside. She held Gabby, who was completely silent in her arms. The small girl had bumped into the fan hard enough that she was unconscious but still breathing. She was bleeding from a lump on her forehead and a cut on her lip.

Bob rushed to the door and let in the paramedic team that had arrived about five minutes after he had called them. They quickly got to Gabby and wasted no time getting her into the ambulance. They were concerned about the large bump on her head and managed to stop the bleeding, which put Christine and Bob at ease. Christine was allowed to ride in the ambulance while Bob followed in their car. When they arrived at the hospital, five ambulances were already lined up waiting to unload. It just so happened that there had been a tour bus accident outside of town and more than fifty people were injured, so the emergency room was packed. They carried Gabby in, hoping to get her help as soon as possible. A young lady dressed in a peppermint-striped outfit saw them and told them to follow her to pediatrics. In the pediatric unit, Dr. Apple immediately saw the bump on Gabby's head so he rushed her into the baby trauma unit.

"Hi, folks, my name is Dr. Apple. I've seen cases like your daughter's before. We will need to operate now to avoid risking any brain damage. Her hematoma is large and could burst. If that happens, we could lose her."

"What are her chances, Doc?" Bob asked, his face flooded with worry.

"Her chances are good if we operate right away. Can we get your approval to do so?"

"Yes. I am her dad, Robert Boral, and this is my wife Christine. Where can we wait?"

"There is a nursery waiting room down this corridor to the right. Please be patient. This could take a few hours."

"We can wait. Can they give us periodic updates on Gabby's progress?"

"Yes. I will have one of our training assistants come out every thirty minutes. Will that be sufficient?"

"Of course. Thank you, Dr. Apple, for helping her so quickly."

"No problem. But if you believe in prayer, start praying. This is a dangerous operation and has about a seventy percent chance of success with no damage. You can call me Nancy from now on."

They all headed to the waiting area while Gabby's operation began. Christine was in distress and replied, "How could I have been so stupid?"

"What are you talking about, Christine?" Bob looked befuddled.

"I forgot to put her crib side panel back up last night before we went to sleep. She must have rolled or fallen right out."

"Honey, it was an easy mistake to make. What I can't figure out is how the fan fell over on her."

"I know. That is odd. Why didn't she scream when she fell out of the bed? It had to hurt."

"Well, for now only God knows for sure. It's not like she can tell us. Let's stop dwelling on that now and start praying for her miracle."

"Yes, dear. May I pray?"

"Please do."

"Father, please forgive me for the mistake I made in forgetting to put the crib panel up. Our baby girl needs Your help right now. We know You can give the doctors direction to help them during the operation, and You can help heal Gabby. We thank you, Father, that through Your son You are answering our prayer. Amen."

Meanwhile, in the emergency room, a rush of more than fifty people was filing in from the bus accident. They consisted of infants to the elderly. All the doctors and nurses were running around trying to take care of each patient. One wounded girl was named Katrina. She was under the age of two and had wounds from head to toe. They were cuts caused by broken glass. The head nurse, Carissa, was called over the loudspeaker to the trauma unit. She was designated to keep watch on Katrina. Upon her arrival at the trauma unit, Carissa saw that Katrina was critically wounded. She called upstairs to check in with Dr. Cutshall. He was busy overseeing Gabby's operation so Carissa called over another doctor to start caring for Katrina. Considering the depth of

Katrina's wounds, they knew her surgery was a matter of life or death.

Back in the waiting area, Bob and Christine began to feel the presence of the Lord.

"Honey, what a wonderful prayer for our lovely daughter. I know the Lord will answer and a miracle will happen," Bob assured his wife.

Four hours later, Gabby was placed in the recovery room while Dr. Cutshall went to the waiting area and updated her parents.

"You two have a very blessed child. Her head wound was so bad that I honestly thought she wouldn't make it. However, during the most critical part of the surgery, the time where most patient's breathing becomes uneven, we witnessed a miracle. Gabby's breathing remained steady. Never have I witnessed this in all my thirty years of practice! Were you praying by any chance?"

"Yes, sir, with all our hearts. And I thank God tremendously for you, and that His hand was with you as well," Christine answered.

"Well, ma'am, to be honest, several months ago we had a baby in our unit who God also gave a miracle to and it changed my life. One of our nurses witnessed a glow in her incubator. After that, she was completely healed of all her troubles. I tell you if that hadn't happened, I'd be even more surprised by today's miracle."

"I totally understand, because the baby you are talking about was our Gabby whom you worked on today."

"Oh my. Well, I don't think there's a word in the dictionary to describe to you how I feel right now."

Just then Dr. Cutshall's name was called over the loudspeaker to come into the trauma unit. He waved good-bye to the Borals. "I'll see you later," he said as he trailed off into the distance.

When he got to the trauma unit, he was told of Katrina's critical condition. Although her operation was a success, she was still barely hanging on for life. He immediately turned to Carissa, "Let's get this baby upstairs to the pediatric unit and put her beside Gabby Boral. There is something special about that girl and I believe God can use her to somehow help this young child."

"I know all about Miss Gabby and I couldn't agree more," she replied with a slight smile creeping onto her face as she turned to do as Dr. Cutshall advised. As soon as Katrina was stabilized, she was unplugged from the station in the trauma unit and placed in the bed next to Gabby's.

Bob and Christine finally got the chance to visit Gabby, who was quickly recovering and now opening her eyes.

"We are so blessed that our daughter is so special. I think that this is just the beginning of what God is going to do through Gabby," Bob commented as Christine immediately nodded in agreement.

"Somehow I know this disaster will turn into another blessing after all." Christine smiled in awe of what God was doing for her.

Just then the head nurse returned to the pediatric unit and asked the Borals for a favor. She knew they were Christians so she felt comfortable asking them to pray with Katrina's parents. The Borals agreed, and they all left together and went downstairs to the trauma unit's waiting area where Katrina's parents were. As they were praying, Katrina was being placed beside Gabby. Gabby was awake and she turned her head to look at Katrina, who was still unconscious and still in danger. Katrina was attached to a special incubator to breathe better. Bob began praying while holding Katrina's father's hand and Christine held Katrina's mother's hand. Katrina's parents were not believers, but were desperate for help and very thankful for the prayer time.

"Dear Father, we thank you in the name of Jesus that you can do what no man can. We pray for little Katrina and her parents, and we ask you to heal her. Please give peace of mind to her parents. We know and trust you to take care of these needs even though we don't know exactly how it will happen. We thank you ahead of time that the answers are coming in Jesus' name. Amen."

Katrina's mother was named Leslie. She thanked Bob for his prayer and then said, "Sir, I know you believe, and I hope that your belief is better than my doubt. My husband and I have already lost two children. One was a miscarriage and the other was stillborn. If we lose our third child, there is no God. But if our child lives, we shall always remember you."

Just then Pastor Elmer entered the room. It just so happened that he had a relative who was in the bus accident. When he saw the Borals, he headed over to them and asked, "How is Gabby doing?"

"She's better," Bob replied. "What are you doing here, Pastor?"

"Oh, my Uncle Jeff was on the bus. He was the driver. I came to visit him and I spotted you."

"How is your Uncle Jeff? Do you know yet?"

"Oh, he is fine. He called me on his cell to let me know that he's doing all right. He says the only thing that hurt was his pride. This was his first accident ever and he feels so guilty that all these people got hurt. Who are these people with you?"

"Nice to meet you, Pastor. We are Mr. and Mrs. Toomey." Leslie held out her hand and then continued. "Our daughter Katrina was wounded very severely in the bus accident and these people prayed with us." She smiled.

"Well, Mr. Toomey, if these people prayed with you, I know God will come through. God has used this family a lot in our church to help many people, and he's already using their little girl to do mighty things," Pastor Elmer responded.

Just then, in the pediatric unit, Gabby instinctively reached her hand toward Katrina's incubator and Katrina opened her eyes. She turned to look at Gabby and started smiling. Gabby then lifted her hands in the air and made some crazy noises. At that very same moment, the head nurse walked by and saw them. "Here she goes again!" she said, rolling her eyes.

Pastor Elmer headed to the room where his uncle was and the two sets of parents went upstairs to the pediatric unit. When they arrived, both babies were awake and smiling. The Toomey's had a rush of joyful tears and the Borals joined them. Dr. Cutshall walked into the room and saw the four parents crying and asked, "Is everything okay?"

"I don't think things could be any better. Our babies are awake and smiling," Bob said, letting the relief of the spirit be known.

"Somehow that doesn't surprise me. Both of these babies are blessed because they both should've died. I'm so glad you've met each other. I know that none of us will ever forget this day. Just for your information, more than twenty people have passed away because of that accident and it's one of the worst disasters we've handled at this hospital. Mr. Toomey, your daughter even had a piece of glass in her that just missed her eye. If it had been any closer to her eye, she would have gone blind in that eye. All I can say is that this is such a miracle."

"Yes, and I think for the first time in my life, I can believe in a God who does miracles through us," Mr. Toomey responded.

"Me, too, honey," Mrs. Toomey agreed. "Let's plan to go to Pastor Elmer's church this Sunday."

During the next several months, both of the Toomeys had accepted Christ and had gotten together with the Borals from time to time. What could possibly happen next in the life of this little gift of God's?

This is A.E. once again, boys and girls, to remind you that Jesus can change all of our lives if we let him. The verse I leave you to think about is located in Mark 10:27.

This chapter is written in honor of all the people involved in healing from traumatic accidents.

Baby Ethan

Just after Gabby had turned three years old, a missionary visited her church from the island of Cebu in the Philippines. Not only did he come as a representative of Compassion International, Reverend Pueblos, also referred to as Big Ray, headed a ministry in Cebu that was spreading like wildfire. He came to the United States searching for volunteers to take a trip to Cebu and help with a current building project. Their greatest outreach was to young people, and Big Ray would be speaking at church that morning to gather other believers who were willing to join the growing ministry. Pastor Elmer introduced him to the congregation and he taught a sermon titled "Go," referencing Matthew 28:19.

Christine kept Gabby with her in church that day because she was leaving early to prepare lunch for Big Ray at the house. Big Ray had a large green sign that he held up that said "Go!" on it. He then began the sermon with:

"Dear people of God, as I preach today when I say the word go, you say go. I'll also have your pastor hold up the sign for me."

The congregation responded with an enthusiastic, "Okay!"

"Let's get started. Go," he said, and the congregation replied with the same.

During his sermon, he used the word "go" thirty times. By the end of the church service, they auctioned off the sign for a fundraiser. The auction ended up raising $2000 for the mission work in Cebu. After the sermon, Christine headed home and began lunch. She knew the Cebu favorites, which included whole tilapia with the heads and eyes still on. She also went to the Asian market that week and bought shrimp with their heads still attached. And she cooked rice pilaf with pancit. She also made sticky rice, a favorite of the children's. When Pastor Elmer, his wife, and Big Ray arrived, Gabby ran to the door and pointed to the missionary, shouting, "Go!"

Big Ray responded with a smile, saying, "You are a quick learner! I believe you need to go to the Philippines."

Then Gabby tugged on his coat with all her might and said, "Me go."

"Excuse my daughter. She is a bit hyper." Christine picked her up and handed her to Bob.

"Nonsense," Big Ray replied. "She is so special. I can see God in her little eyes. Please take her to Cebu. I have a family that would love to meet her."

Bob replied, " I don't know if that's in God's plans for us. My wife would love to go, but with Gabby that may be too much."

"I believe Jesus will use your family greatly to encourage other families in my church, so please consider it."

"Please come to lunch. I have a Philippine treat for you," Christine's excited voice echoed through to the living room where the men were still talking.

During the meal, they discussed the mission trip and its three-week stay. This would consist of hard work and meeting many people. Christine turned to Gabby and said, "Gabby, you can go to your playroom now."

"Me go now." Gabby looked at Big Ray with round eyes full of energy.

He looked into her eyes and then began praying. "I love this child! I pray in Jesus' name that you will be a blessing to everyone you meet in your life. You are already such a blessing I can see."

"Thank you, Pastor. We will find a way to let her come to your church." Bob smiled from ear to ear.

Gabby went to her playroom and the adults chatted for another hour. Pastor Elmer closed in prayer. When they were ready to leave, Gabby heard them saying goodbyes and cried, saying, "Me go! Me go!"

Pastor Ray looked at her and said, "You WILL go. Later."

After they left, Christine calmed Gabby down. An hour later Elder Lambert visited. He had the 'Go' sign in his hand.

"God told me to give this sign to your family. Christine, an hour after church the Lord said to give it to you. I don't know why, but here it is."

"Thank you, Mr. Lambert. I believe it is for Gabby."

The moment Gabby saw the sign she said, "See! Me go! Me go!" That was a prophetic word from a three-year-old.

"She knows the sign?" Mr. Lambert asked.

Nodding her head and pointing to the sign, Gabby said, "Yes, me go! ME GO!" getting louder with each word.

"Gabby has been saying that ever since church was over. I think she is determined to go to Cebu," Bob said.

"Well, after church, two thousand dollars was raised from the sign. Pastor Pueblos wants to give half of the money for someone to go to the Philippines. I believe

God is sending you, Christine, and Gabby. I'll discuss this with the deacon board and I'm sure they'll approve."

"Brother Lambert, that is such a nice offer. God is already preparing the way," Bob replied.

"I need to ask God for my half yet, but I know it will come," Christine added.

"No problem. I will tell that to the board as well on Tuesday night."

Bob led Brother Lambert to his study to discuss a few other church matters. Christine took Gabby to her room, where they played together until Gabby took her nap. That night, there was a ladies auxiliary meeting. Janice Myers led the meeting discussing how they could help for the Cebu trip. Janice's daughter Julie read the notes from their last meeting and gave the financial report. "There was a total of $1000 in the fund. And we will now take suggestions as to how it should be spent." Next, Elder Lambert's wife spoke up.

"My husband was at the Boral house today. He shared the excitement of Christine and Gabby possibly going to Cebu. I suggest that we give the $1000 toward their trip."

Mrs. Beyers motioned and Mrs. Paulson seconded. They then opened a vote and it was a unanimous yes.

"Christine, I will tell my husband and they will vote on this as well at their Tuesday meeting," Mrs. Lambert concluded.

Tears of joy began welling in her eyes as Christine responded, "I can't comprehend all this. To God be the glory!" When the meeting ended, Christine rushed home to share the news with Bob.

On Tuesday, when Elder Lambert brought up the Borals' desire to join the Cebu trip, they took a vote with Elder Joel Fort motioning the approval. Suddenly, a voice spoke up form the back of the room.

"Dear fellow board members. It is with my deepest thoughts and prayers that this family must go to the Philippines. We have all been touched by Gabby's life. I believe great things will come from this trip as well," Pastor Elmer said with great emotional support.

Immediately following his announcement, Elder Meyers seconded the motion and the vote was won with almost all yeses. Within the next month, another $2000 was donated toward the Borals' trip to Cebu from several sources, so the Borals placed the order for their tickets.

After several days, Pastor Pueblos heard the news and set up a schedule for the members who had signed up for the Cebu trip. They would arrive just before July 4.

On the day of departure, Gabby kissed her "GO" sign and her dad. The flight took twenty-two hours and included boarding three different planes. When they landed in Cebu, Gabby said, "Me go? Me here!"

As they departed the plane, Pastor Pueblos, Elluis, Melody Invento, and several other helpers from Compassion International greeted them.

"Hello and welcome to Cebu. We welcome you as our honored guests. I am Pastor Pueblos and this is my wife Stella. We are glad that you have arrived safely and are looking forward to working with you."

"My name is Melanie and I work with Compassion International. My friend Romeo and I will be your guides during your visit. I am the sister of Melody here, and this is her husband Elluis."

"Baby! Purtty baby!" Gabby exclaimed seeing a baby in Melody's arms.

"You must be Gabby. This is Ethan, my nephew." Ethan looked at Gabby and laughed in approval at the ribbon in her hair. They all climbed into the church bus and headed for the church. On the way to the church, Pastor Pueblos gave them all a schedule for the next three weeks. In the schedule was a building project for a youth center that would seat 300 youth. Also scheduled were a few sightseeing visits.

The Waltermyer family was also along for the trip. Bill, the husband, would be helping with the construction while Liezyl and her children were staying with the rest of her family who lived in Cebu. At the church, another greeting committee awaited their arrival. "Welcome, our American friends. We are excited to have you here," Liezyl's brother John Ray announced. He was in a wheelchair due to a crippling bone disease, yet was still as chipper as ever even though doctors had predicted his death five years ago. Standing beside him were several others in their family, their friend Emily, and twenty members from their church. Eventually, after being fed and acquainted with all the new faces, the tourists rested at their places for the evening.

During the day, Gabby stayed in a playroom in the Compassion International office building. Melody offered to take care of her personal needs because she was already watching her son Ethan during the day. Ethan was born with a hole in his heart and desperately needed surgery, which would cost $25,000, or one million pesos of Philippine money. They didn't have that kind of money, or even insurance to help them. As soon as Christine found this out, she decided to meet with them and pray. When she arrived at their home, she said, "I'm so sorry to hear about your son's condition, but I am here today to pray and believe in God for a miracle."

"We need a miracle for our son. Ethan is so full of life and joy. This operation will save his life and give us more time to enjoy his joyful spirit," Elluis added.

Christine smiled. "I believe God can provide that with no problem. We just need to ask and believe." So she began to pray, "Dear Father, I thank You that Your son Jesus is truly our provider. I thank You now for providing for this family the miracle for their son. You know how to do it and I know You will do it! In Jesus' name we believe! Amen." She then looked to Melody and Elluis saying, "I will contact our prayer team back home. And they will start praying right away for Ethan. I just know that God will answer." Christine then said good-bye and headed to the site where the church was being built. She would be in charge of overseeing the lunch preparation and meal cleanup for each day at the building project.

The next day in the playroom of the Compassion building, Gabby found blocks with letters on them. Even though she hadn't learned how to spell yet, she spelled a word without knowing it. It was the word 'heal.' When Melody saw the word, she yelled, "Everyone come here. You must see this!" The staff all came rushing in and were in awe of the sight before their eyes. A three-year-old had spelled the word "heal." It was absolutely prophetic.

"I want a picture of that. Let's take it before she tears it down. We will hang it up for everyone to see!" Pastor Wenefredo spoke this with loads of excitement.

Just then Gabby pointed to the blocks, saying, "Baby." It was as if she knew the word she spelled was meant for Ethan.

Meanwhile, at the work site, the men were laying the foundation down. Bill Waltermyer was hauling the blocks on a flatbed cart along with Romeo. The building would be 100 feet long and 20 feet wide. Several churches from the United States had donated plenty of materials. By using volunteers, the savings would be immense for the church. There were a total of fourteen churches represented in the group of over 100 workers. During the construction, several opportunities arose to share Jesus with some of the volunteers who weren't believers. News spread and more helpers came daily. Each day, Pastor Elmer lead a few worship songs with the help of Melanie and the youth choir. Christine fulfilled her promise and called back home to get a prayer chain started for Ethan. Even though Gabby didn't understand, she knew something was going on with Ethan. Every chance she got to be with him, she'd make him laugh. On the third day of construction, Bill Waltermeyer led a man to the Lord. By the end of day four, the foundation was finished and one wall was almost complete.

"Dear fellow laborers, I can't express my gratitude enough for your help to make this building possible. As pastor here, I wish to reach out to all of you in any way that will bless you for your help." Pastor Wenefredo took a deep breath and continued with, "The first miracle we are believing is for Ethan Invento to get his surgery and continuing to live a joyful life with us. Tomorrow we are going to spend a few moments in prayer on that."

The next day at the construction site all the workers got together to pray for Ethan. They prayed in faith, and by the end of the prayer a voice spoke out very boldly. "It will happen!" Everyone turned around to see John Ray, the crippled boy, with a great joyous expression on his face. The group then began to sing a chorus of Amen. At the end of the song you could hear people saying, "It is done." Or adding another "Amen!"

By the end of week two, the entire outer structure of the youth building was complete. The last week would include the inside work of painting and plumbing. Just three days before the end of the third week, a truck full of school supplies arrived that were donated from fifty different churches in the United States. On the last day of the trip, Christine woke up and opened her laptop. As she was checking her emails, she noticed that someone in the prayer chain had heard from a doctor in San Francisco who committed to donating his time to come and operate on Ethan. Christine jumped up and ran outside as quickly as she could and began sharing the word with everyone. "It is my pleasure to announce that a doctor from America has offered to operate on Ethan! And all the finances are being paid for by an organization!" Everyone rejoiced and praised God.

That evening, when it was time for all the visitors to go back home, Gabby kissed Ethan and said, "You go! Be well."

As the plane left, little Ethan looked to the sky and pointed. He laughed as if to say thank you to Gabby and the other volunteers.

Knowing that Ethan's heart surgery was paid for inspired the entire congregation. The money that had been raised for Ethan prior to the other organization covering the cost was donated to help other needy children. That fall Ethan had his surgery, and to this day he is fully healthy and living a normal, jolly life.

This story reminds me that God always gives good gifts to those who are in need. This is A.E. inspiring you to remember how God provides just like the Bible says in Matthew 7:22.

This chapter is in honor of the Invento family from Cebu, Philippines.

Kindergarten

It was August 25. Gabby had turned five years old and she was facing a new adventure. That's right, kindergarten. Gabby had been to her neighborhood school many times before. She had often played on the schoolyard playground with her parents or Mary Delone, the school safety monitor for her street. Mary's job was to accompany the elementary students as they walked to school during the school year. By 8:30 a.m., Mary and about ten other students from the neighborhood came by to pick up Gabby for the very first time. Gabby was so excited as she headed out that she jumped down from the last two steps and hugged Mary. She then got in line and headed next door with the group. Mike Gross came marching out and joined the line of students, just about as excited as all the other young children. He skipped into place as he took the last spot in line.

When they reached the intersection between the school and Gabby's block, the crossing guard named Charlotte May held up her stop sign to traffic, allowing everyone to cross. Gabby looked at this bright-haired woman, smiled, and said, "Thank you, lady! I'm Gabby Boral!"

Wiping the sweat from her brow, Charlotte replied, "Nice to meet you, Gabby. Enjoy your first day at school!"

Gabby remembered her mom's last words as she entered the school: "You're going to school, but not to play on the playground. You're going to learn." Gabby smiled to herself and gladly accepted that something new was happening today. She stood tall and thought about how much bigger she must be. *I'm going to school just like all the other kids!* As they approached the school, Gabby was led to her new classroom and met her new teacher, Mrs. Miller, an elderly lady near retirement age. She had salt and pepper hair and wore glasses. Mrs. Miller started the day by introducing herself. "Hello! I'm Mrs. Miller, your teacher. You will learn many things here and we will get to know each other. I have one rule. That is to listen and learn, and if you don't listen, you won't learn, and that would make me sad."

Just then, Gabby noticed a boy in the back right corner of the room who decided to make some trouble. He started off the day by putting a worm on the desk of the girl who sat in front of him. "Yikes!" she screamed.

Her black hair bounced around as she flew from the desk, accidentally pushing her chair to the floor. The whole class began to roar with laughter and Mrs. Miller sought to correct the situation.

"These kinds of actions won't help us to learn. You, young man, get to learn a lesson really quickly! Now go over and stand in that corner," she said while pointing to a windowsill with peeling paint and many dead bugs on it. Mrs. Miller then tossed the worm out the window, and a minute later a robin swooped in to make a meal of it. George behaved the rest of that day. Yet many of his sneaky actions were to come.

During the morning lesson, the class began learning the alphabet. Mrs. Miller had many objects she used to teach. That day she began with the first five letters.

"Our first letter is A," she announced, holding up a fruit. "Does anyone know what this fruit is?"

Gabby shouted, "A delicious red apple!"

"Very good! What is your name?"

"Gabby Boral."

"Because you answered correctly, you get to keep the apple. You may come get it when school is over."

Gabby smiled and said, "Thank you, but I can't take food from strangers."

"Well, that's a good point. We won't be strangers for long. You will be here for the next 180 school days so you will know me very well."

Mrs. Miller continued with the letter B, holding up a baseball bat, and then the letter C, showing a picture of her pet cat. For the letter D, she showed a picture of a dog. And then she concluded with the picture of an elephant for the letter E. Gabby was so glad she didn't bring in a live animal for each. There would have been no room left in the classroom!

The day flew by and before they knew it, it was lunch followed by recess. During the first recess, Gabby rushed to the swing. Just as she was about to sit, she was pushed to the ground from behind.

"Who pushed me?" Gabby asked angrily.

"I did! What are you gonna do about it?" said a third grader whose name was Alexia.

"I'll tell my mommy on you."

"Oh, a mommy's little baby! Are you wearing your diapers today? Do you need to be changed?" Just then, Alexia fell to the ground, and behind her stood a bigger girl named Felicia.

"Push someone your own size around, brat!" she said. "Here, little girl! You can sit and swing now." She patted the swing and helped Gabby up. Alexia got up and rushed off, and Felicia introduced herself. "My name is

Felicia, but most people call me Felix. And if Alexia ever bothers you again, just let me know. I'll take care of her." She paused to make a fist and pounded it into her open palm. "What's your name?"

"I'm Gabby Boral. Thank you, but what you did wasn't necessary."

"Oh, yes it was! Alexia tries every year to find someone to pick on and I rescue them. You enjoy the rest of your day. I'll see ya around," she said and confidently stepped away in her own rhythm.

Soon the bell rang and recess was over. Everyone filed into a line and headed back to the classroom. It was now time for math class. Christine had taught Gabby enough about math that she could already count to 100 and do easy addition. Mrs. Miller saw how quick Gabby was with math and wanted to give her more advanced math to do. When school ended that day and Gabby came up front for her red apple, Mrs. Miller said, "Gabby, you are very good at math. Did your mother teach you all that at home?"

"Yes! I can count to 100 and do lots of adding problems. Is that going to be a problem, Mrs. Miller?"

"No, it's quite a blessing. I think you need to jump to first grade math. I'll need to talk to the principal and your parents about it. Is that okay with you?"

"Yes, ma'am! I'll even tell you my parents' phone numbers. They both have cell phones."

"That's great. I'll call them tonight."

"Okay, but please call after seven o'clock because we have supper time."

"Fine. Thank you, Gabby."

"You're welcome. I need to get to my safety to get home. Good-bye! I'll see you tomorrow!"

Immediately after Gabby left, Mrs. Miller went to Principal Platts' office to tell him the news about Gabby. When she entered his office, he grinned and said, "I was expecting you." He was a short, big-bellied, dark-haired man with glasses, and usually a pleasant man who was easy to talk to.

"What do you mean you were expecting me, sir?"

"Do you have a girl in your class named Gabby Boral?"

"Yes! I came to talk to you about her." Mrs. Miller had a surprised glint in her eyes.

"I know. I have the complaint right here in front of me."

"Complaint?"

"She was in a fight today. And the other girl got hurt. Alexia Brown fell on the ground and landed on a nail that went into her buttocks."

"Mr. Platts, this girl seems too nice to have done that. She's very smart and doesn't appear to be the bully type."

"I'll take that into consideration. However, I must do my job. I'm going to follow up on this story with all the parents and students."

"Were there any witnesses?" a confused Mrs. Miller asked.

"Yes. Felicia Jones said she saw the whole thing. I have her story already. This situation must be addressed."

Meanwhile, Gabby arrived at home and her parents asked how her first day went. "It was great!" Gabby said, forgetting all about recess. "You're going to get a phone call from my teacher about how great it was."

"That's wonderful." Christine smiled. "Supper is ready and I made your favorite. Macaroni and cheese with pigs in a blanket."

They all ate dinner and Gabby stared closely at the clock. At 6:45 the phone rang.

"Hello," answered Bob. As the phone call continued, the expression on his face changed from an even-toned expression to dismay, and then a horrified, wide-eyed expression appeared before vanishing again. "Okay. We'll see you in fifteen minutes," Bob said as he ended the call. He glanced over at Gabby with an uneasy expression. With a puzzled frown, he called Christine over to the front door and said in a quiet tone of voice, "Christine, the principal and Gabby's teacher are on their way over.

Something happened at school with Gabby today and they need to talk to us about it."

"Okay." Christine nodded and went back to the table to finish cleaning up supper. She dismissed Gabby from putting her dirty dishes into the dishwasher and then asked her to go to her room. Bob stiffly tucked in his chair and assisted his wife in the kitchen, cleaning up until the doorbell rang at seven o'clock. He answered with an introduction of himself and his wife, who offered refreshments.

"Just water or a soda will be fine," Mr. Platts said. "This is Gabby's teacher Mrs. Miller." He motioned to Mrs. Miller.

"To what do we owe this pleasure of meeting you both?" Bob inquired.

"I wish it were a pleasure. A fight occurred today on the playground during recess and Gabby was involved."

"Mr. Platts, I know my daughter didn't start a fight. We've taught her that's wrong."

"I'm not questioning you, sir. Where is your daughter?"

"Gabby, you have visitors. Please come down and sit beside your mom and me," Bob called.

Gabby ran down the stairs so quickly it almost could have been mistaken for a herd of elephants invading the house. She saw Mrs. Miller, and delighted, said, "I thought it was you! Have you told my parents the good news?"

"Good news?" her dad said, dragging out the words as they came.

"Gabby, sit down here and listen. You know Mrs. Miller, and this is Mr. Platts, the principal."

"I know. She told that me she would tell him. Nice to meet you Mr. Platts."

"You seem pleased about this meeting, young lady. However, we're not. And you're in trouble," said Mr. Platts.

"I just did good in math class. What's wrong with that?"

"I told the principal about that, but he told me something bad about you in return," replied Mrs. Miller.

"What did I do?"

"Gabby, you mean you don't know what they're talking about?" Christine said with a puzzled look on her face.

"No. The one bad thing that happened today was one girl pushed me down and then another girl pushed her down."

"What? Who pushed who?" Mr. Platts interrupted, sounding even angrier as the conversation continued.

"Sir, a girl named Alexia pushed me down. And then Felicia pushed her down. And Felicia told me that if she ever does it again, I am to tell her and she'll take care of Alexia."

"Well we were told a different story. Alexia fell on a nail, got up, and ran away. And Felicia said she saw the whole thing. That you pushed Alexia down."

"They're both liars!"

"Gabby, we want the truth here. We will investigate all sides of this story."

"Mr. Platts, my daughter has never been a liar. We trust this situation can be resolved quickly."

"Mr. Boral, I assure you we want the same thing."

"We have now heard three sides of the story and will call a meeting with all the families a week from now. Thank you for your time. I will be calling you."

"Gabby, I want you to know that if we find you innocent of this matter, we will discuss the math situation later. Mr. Platts and I have already discussed it today." Mrs. Miller also nodded her head toward Gabby's parents before exiting the house.

That night, the Borals led a prayer over the situation and then sent Gabby to bed.

Over the next three days, Gabby avoided the other girls who were involved and stayed very quiet about it. Mrs. Miller saw the way Gabby handled herself and found it quite admirable. The other two girls, however, were a different story. They continued to spread rumors to the entire school. Gabby's church friends who also attended Goodman Elementary started to avoid her.

Then another interesting thing happened. Felicia began bringing in new items. First it was a new smartphone, then a twenty-dollar necklace, and even new shoes. Alexia used to show off her new stuff, but now every morning it was becoming more and more common to see Felicia showing off new items. A week passed and Principal Platts called in all the parents and students involved for a meeting in his office at 7:00 p.m. Saturday evening. First Alexia told her side, pointing to a pair of jeans with a hole in them as she scolded Gabby and declared, "It's all *your* fault!"

Felicia was next to speak. "I rescued Alexia from that little brat." She pointed at Gabby and then stuck her nose in the air.

Finally, Gabby spoke. "This is all one big lie and I can prove it!" The other girls looked at her as their jaws dropped and the parents simply observed. "Mr. Platts, my teacher Mrs. Miller told you something else about me, didn't she?" Gabby began.

"Well, yes, but that means nothing in this situation," he replied.

"If you would excuse me, sir, I think it does," Gabby politely went on. "If you were about to get a prize for doing something good, would you do something bad to stop it?"

"Not usually." Mr. Platts began to look confused.

"However, sir, if you do something wrong and get a prize, is that good?"

"No." He scratched his chin and then asked, "What's your point?"

"Why don't you ask Felicia where she's getting all of her new gifts from?"

Felicia's mother Nancy butted in and asked, "Yeah, who is giving you all these new items? I found a new dress in your room yesterday and we sure didn't buy it for you."

Alexia immediately got up and asked to go to the restroom.

"Come to think of it, daughter, I found my hidden money spot empty the other day. Three hundred dollars is missing. Do you know anything about that?" She turned and cocked her head, looking directly at her daughter Alexia.

"No, Mom." Alexia's eyes widened. She crossed her legs and emphasized, "I have to go really bad."

"Go, young lady," Mr. Platts interrupted, "but you come right back as soon as you're done."

As soon as Alexia left the room, Felicia spoke up. "Sir, I have something to say."

"Yes? What is it?" Mr. Platts looked ready to listen.

"Alexia bribed me by giving me all these gifts so I wouldn't tell the truth. What Gabby said is true. I lied so I could get more gifts, and got innocent Gabby in trouble." She rested her head, angling it closer to the ground in dismay.

"Well, how about that," Mr. Platts stated. "Here's what we're going to do to solve this." He pointed his finger in the air as a solution came to mind.

"What happened?" Alexia asked as she entered the room trying to look innocent.

"I think you, young lady, must confess like Miss Felicia here did and apologize to Gabby," Mr. Platts added.

"You backstabber, Felix! I hate you!" Alexia scowled at Felicia.

"That's enough out of you!" her mother scolded. "Mr. Platts, I'm sorry for my daughter's actions. What did you have in mind for punishment?"

"First, I think Felicia must give all these gifts back to you, Mrs. Matthews." Mr. Platts nodded at Alexia's mother. "And then you can try to get your money back. Also, Alexia, you will receive a three day suspension from school." He looked toward her as her shoulders hunched over. "Third," he announced and turned to the others, "Gabby will get her reward of learning a higher level of math." He smiled at Gabby. "And lastly, you all must shake hands and forgive one another." Mr. Platts rested his gaze on all three students and then nodded to himself.

"Mr. Platts?"

"Yes, Gabby?"

"Please don't suspend Alexia. Give her a second chance to turn things around. Besides, maybe she'll learn that being a bully usually backfires."

"That's a nice thought, Gabby. What punishment do you think these girls should get?"

Mrs. Miller jumped in. "I think we can give them some cleaning chores to do as payment."

"I've got it!" Mr. Platts again stuck his finger in the air. "We will have you both clean the slides and swings off after a rain, and you must hold the doors for all the children after recess all month long."

The two girls exchanged looks of dismay, and then Alexia added, "I guess it's better than being suspended. I'm sorry, Gabby."

"I forgive you."

"I'm sorry, too," Felicia said. "I shouldn't have let money convince me not to do the right thing."

"I forgive you, too." Gabby nodded.

"By the way, children. I once got in trouble in fourth grade for cheating on a test. I had to clean all the chalkboards for a whole month. But look where I am today," Mr. Platts said with encouragement.

The meeting came to an end as the parents had their children apologized. Before she left, Gabby told Alexia and Felicia about Jesus. Both felt so guilty that they agreed to go to church with her on Sunday. The Sunday school lesson was on Matthew 18:21-35 where Jesus talked about forgiving sins and debts. By the end of that class, both girls wanted to give their hearts to Jesus, and they thanked Gabby for being so forgiving.

"I know Jesus forgives everyone, and he wants me to do the same thing. I'm glad you came to church with me." Gabby smiled.

The rest of that year, Felicia and Alexia always watched out for Gabby, and if any bullies were around, they would remember the story of Jesus' forgiveness of the man in debt. Many more children were invited to Sunday school because of Gabby's willingness to be kind and tell about Jesus. Boys and girls, this is A.E. inviting you to read the parable of forgiveness with your parents in Matthew 18:21-35.

This chapter is dedicated to Mrs. Miller, Allen's first grade teacher, and Mr. Platts, a principal at his school.

The Uncle Next Door

When Gabby turned six years old, her Uncle Roy moved in next door. He was known as the candy man. He always had a candy dish on the table for the neighborhood children to enjoy. Uncle Roy had a workshop in the backyard and lots of trees, including three apple trees that always had net caterpillars each year. He also had a wooden arch that was used for a grapevine, which was always filled with red grapes and many yellow jackets flying around. One day while he was riding his mower, he saw Gabby playing on her teeter-totter.

"What are you doing, Gabby?"

"Hi, Uncle Roy! Waiting for the neighborhood girls to come over so we can bounce on this thing together."

"Okay. Have fun. I have to finish mowing, and then I'll spray the caterpillar nests."

"Oh, does that kill 'em?"

"Yes, Gabby, but rather dead caterpillars than a dead apple tree. You like apples, don't you?"

"Yes, sir, I do. Can I have one before you spray?"

"I'll pick one for each of your family members. Talk to you later."

Soon the neighbor girls, Joni and Jeana and Corinne, came over and played for two hours. When Uncle Roy dropped off the apples, he asked Bob a question.

"How would you like to help me with a project in my workshop?"

"I would love to. What are we working on?"

"It's a secret. Don't tell anybody." Uncle Roy was famous for always doing a project in his shop. He would build sleds and lots of things made of wood. But this time he was very quiet about what he was doing. "Bob you can't tell anyone about this project because this is a special one that I hope lasts a lifetime."

"Okay. I'll be over when I'm finished with a project I'm working on. Give me about three hours."

"Dad, what did Uncle Roy want?" Gabby peered out the living room door that Bob was about to close.

"He wants me to come over and work on a project in his workshop. But he told me it's a secret."

"Aw, Daddy, I'm your little girl and I can keep a secret. What's Uncle Roy working on?"

"Sweetie, a promise is a promise, but I will tell you this. We plan to have it done by Thanksgiving. So be patient."

"Oh, but, Daddy, that's three months away. I can't wait that long."

"Gabby, remember what the book of James says. Patience is a virtue."

"Okay. I know whatever it is it will be big and beautiful."

They all went to bed that night and Gabby lay down for about an hour, thinking about what the project might be. First she thought *a boat,* because Uncle Roy liked to fish. Next she thought *a dollhouse for me,* because Uncle Roy liked Gabby and had no children of his own. His wife Carrie died many years before and couldn't have children. So after several more thoughts, Gabby dozed off into a dreamland and slept through the rest of the night. When she woke up the next morning, she thought about it all over again. She came up with a plan to get someone taller to put her on his or her shoulders so that she could peek into the window. *I know. I'll get Mr. Martin to lift me. He is a nice man,* Gabby thought as she smiled to herself. Mr. Martin lived four houses up the street. He was a quiet man, but still very kind. Gabby waited until after school to go to his house. Mrs. Martin answered the door.

"Hi, Gabby. What brings you here today?"

"Mrs. Martin, I wondered if your husband could do me a favor."

"What kind of favor?"

"Well, I want to peek inside Uncle Roy's shop to see what he's working on."

"Oh, curiosity is bothering you, huh? Well, Mr. Martin is out of town for a week. However, Roy told all of us grownups not to let any of the children in the neighborhood know what the project was. I suggest you just wait until its finished."

"Okay, but it just has me wondering why it's such a secret this time."

"I believe it will be a big surprise, and that's what he wants. If you wait, it will be worth it."

"Thank you, Mrs. Martin. I will wait. God will make it worthwhile."

Mrs. Martin watched Gabby step through the yards and go home as she stared at the workshop the whole way. A month passed and Halloween was just around the corner. Gabby liked to see all the other children in their costumes, but knew it was an evil celebration and she wouldn't celebrate it. There were always bad people pulling tricks. Last year two boys knocked over an old outhouse while a man was sitting inside of it. The year before that, someone tossed toilet paper onto every pine tree on the street. One girl even got a bad piece of candy that made her sick and she almost died. Gabby's family continued the ritual of putting up Christmas decorations a week before Halloween to think about Jesus instead of the evil time.

It was October 24 and Bob and Christine had just tucked Gabby in for the night. An hour later they heard a loud bang outside. The whole neighborhood heard it and everyone looked out their windows. "Oh no!" screamed Christine frantically. "Uncle Roy's workshop is on fire! Bob, call 911. I'll go check on Uncle Roy." Christine quickly threw a robe over her nightgown and headed straight for the workshop. Uncle Roy had been known to work late nights in his shop.

"Hey! Hey! Over here!" Roy waved an arm and Christine met him halfway to the door.

"Oh my! Uncle Roy! Are you okay?" Christine asked as he began deeply sobbing and clenching his chest.

After several deep breaths, Roy replied, "I'm just so upset to see my shop on fire. Who could do such a thing?"

"I don't know, but the fire trucks are here now and the men can hopefully save your shop."

"It's not the shop I'm worried about but my project for the children."

"I'm sure that they will try to save all that they can." Just then a fire marshal came to Roy's porch, where he and Christine had made it safely away from the fire.

"Hi, Roy, are you okay?" he asked.

"I am, but how is the shop?" he asked worriedly.

"Well, it looks like we can save the outside, but the inside is in pretty bad shape. One thing is odd, though."

"What's that?"

"The project you were working on seems to be untouched. I found this book on top of it with a note attached."

"Let me see it. Oh, it's a Bible and the note says, 'God, guard this project with your hand and let it become a blessing to all who use it in Jesus' name. Amen.'"

"Roy! God did just that! Everything else is charred and burned. But that big, gray cover acted as a shield. You are a blessed man," the fireman responded. "Let's go inside where it's warmer so we can talk some more."

They headed inside where Christine offered to make hot chocolate, which was Uncle Roy's favorite drink. Just as they were getting settled in, a knock was heard on the front door. Uncle Roy answered it. There was a man and a boy whom he did not recognize. The boy was about eleven years old and was crying as he said, "Sir, my name is Danny and I owe you an apology. I was hiding by your woodpile under the shop, playing with my dad's blowtorch. Before I knew it, a spark caught fire near your mower and I got scared and I ran to my dad. I'm so sorry, sir, the fire was all my fault."

Beside Danny stood his father Mark, who also began apologizing. "I'm so sorry for my son's actions. He has something he wants to ask you. Go ahead, son. Ask."

"Sir, I want to know what happened to the man that was inside the building."

The fire marshal then spoke up, alarmed. "A man inside? What man inside? We have no evidence of anyone being in there."

Everyone then looked to Uncle Roy, who had been near the area before the fire. With an equally shocked look on his face, he replied, "There's no way anyone could have been inside. I locked the door when I left and nobody was there." He looked even more puzzled when he finished his sentence.

Before anyone could think, the door flew open. "Uncle Roy, are you okay?" Gabby waltzed in with hair resembling a woolly mammoth and pajamas that were put on backward.

Everyone exhaled a sigh of relief and Christine's hand flew over her heart as she exclaimed,

"Oh, thank goodness, Gabby. I thought you were still in bed, but since you're already here you can come sit with me as we figure this all out."

Simultaneously, Uncle Roy looked up and smiled at her. As soon as Christine had finished, he added, "Yes, Gabby, I'm fine. Thank you."

Her eyes wandered to his hand where he was still holding the Bible. "Uncle Roy, what are you doing with my Bible?"

"It's yours?"

"Yeah, look inside the back cover and you'll find my name there. I've been looking for it for days."

Just then Bob entered the room, staring at Gabby and the Bible. "Thank God," he said. "I left your Bible in the shop three days ago and forgot to get it, Gabby."

"It's a blessing it didn't burn," added Uncle Roy.

"Oh, I know why," replied the woolly mammoth. "I asked Jesus to guard it wherever it was. So he did!" Gabby said.

"He sure did, and I believe he was in my shop protecting it and my sleigh."

"Sleigh?" Gabby's eyes grew wider. "Is that the project you were working on?"

"Yes, Gabby, I've been building a sleigh for all of you children to ride on when it snows this winter."

"Wow, that's great! And Jesus protected it, didn't He?" She had a look of excitement in her eyes.

"He sure did, and I'm starting to wonder about that man Danny here says he saw."

"Oh. why of course!" Gabby exclaimed, beaming now. "That was Jesus making sure that the fire didn't hurt the sleigh or my Bible."

Everyone joined hands and began to pray and thank God. Not only had He spared the sleigh and Bible, but Uncle Roy and Danny were perfectly safe, too.

Uncle Roy's secret about the sleigh was now out, but the blessing of how it was protected traveled all throughout the town. It was displayed in Uncle Roy's front yard every year until he died. Many children had their pictures taken on the sleigh, and that winter a big snowstorm came and Roy was giving plenty of rides to the children. Jesus is truly the savior of our lives and the things that we love. And remember, boys and girls, we can bless other children with what we are given. This is A.E. signing off with our scripture reading in Psalm 91. God Bless.

This story was written in the memory of Uncle Roy's sleigh in the front yard in Weigelstown, Pennsylvania.

Faith Without Sight

One Sunday morning, Pastor Elmer had a new membership welcoming service. Seven families were brought into membership that day and included a total of thirteen young people. After the service, there was a fellowship meal in honor of the new members. The idea behind this was to help them get acquainted with the rest of the church members. The pastor's wife Beth brought one of the families over to the table where the Borals were sitting.

"Bob and Christine, I want you to meet the Keeney family. This is Phil and his wife Kelly, and these are their daughters Angela, Bobby Jo, and Cheyenne."

"It's a pleasure to meet you all. I am Bob Boral. This is my wife Christine, and our daughter Gabby."

"It's nice to also meet you. My three daughters are excited about the youth activities going on here. Cheyenne, my youngest, is blind and very active."

"How did she become blind, sir?" Gabby asked, being nosey as usual.

"She accidentally got a container of fluid spilled over her at the age of three and it blinded her permanently."

"Sorry for my daughter's outburst. She tends to speak before she thinks."

"No problem, sir. It happens a lot. However, Cheyenne is very good at one thing most people aren't. Since being blinded, her sense of hearing has gotten a lot stronger. She once heard a small tapping sound that we didn't hear and it saved us a ton of money. It turned out that there was a squirrel in our attic chewing on a wire. I followed her direction to the sound and found the chewed wire which could have caused a fire if I hadn't caught it in time. Then I sealed up the hole that he had found to come inside."

"WOW!" Gabby announced with bulging eyes. "What a gift! I wish I could hear that well."

"It's a proven fact, Gabby, that when a person loses one sense, another one gets stronger. I've also heard that you already have a sense of your own. Rumors have it that you're sensitive to the Holy Spirit and that's an even better gift."

"Thank you, sir. It's entirely the Lord. I just try to listen."

"You sound like a cool girl, Gabby. I hope you and I can become friends," Cheyenne chimed in with a smile.

"My exact thoughts. Can Cheyenne come over to play at our house today, sir?" Gabby asked Mr. Keeney.

"Gabby, not so fast. We just met them. Give them time to get acquainted," her mother responded.

"As a matter of fact, Cheyenne needs friends. If it's okay, we will bring her over today."

"All right, Phil. How does three o'clock sound? Would that be fine with you?" Bob answered.

"That's fine by me. We'll see you then. One question, though. Gabby, what do you plan to do? Cheyenne is limited in what she does."

"I just got some new doll accessories and a new dollhouse. She can hold the dolls while I arrange my house."

"That sounds like fun, Dad. I can hardly wait!" Cheyenne exclaimed.

"Yes, daughter. We will go. And you will take your new doll with you also."

Time passed quickly and soon it was three o'clock. Right then, the Keeney's pulled into Gabby's driveway. Gabby was already peering out the window and ran outside to meet Cheyenne. Cheyenne was wearing a bright red dress and holding a doll in her arms.

"What's your doll's name, Cheyenne?" Gabby asked eagerly.

"I named her Rebecca. May we see your doll house now?"

"See?"

"Hah! A figure of speech. Let me get my guide stick and you lead the way." Cheyenne smiled at her.

"Ahh. I see you have a sense of humor. I like that. Let me hold your doll and guide you with my other hand."

"That's not necessary. I have my stick. I'll just follow your voice and you can lead me that way."

Before Cheyenne's family left, her mom said, "Have a good time. We will be back by six o'clock to pick you up."

"Okay, Mom." Cheyenne and Gabby waved and then they went inside to Gabby's room. Gabby was amazed at how quickly Cheyenne found her way around.

The dollhouse was huge. It was three feet tall by four feet wide. Next to it was Gabby's bed, which Cheyenne used to place her things on. Cheyenne had brought along a bag that was draped across her shoulder and she had filled it with some extra doll clothes. Gabby watched as Cheyenne pulled the clothes out of the bag and began dressing her doll.

"Wow! You can change those clothes pretty quickly for somebody who can't see. Do you go just by feeling what you're doing?"

"Partly, yes, but I also have a special method. When I pack the clothes, I place them in a certain order so that when I take them out, I know which piece is coming next."

"Wow, that's pretty clever. You must be good at memorizing."

"Oh, yes. I can tell you already that you have twelve stairs between your first and second floor."

"I never thought about counting steps, but I can see where that can come in handy, especially if you're entering a house for the first time."

They continued talking and playing. Before they knew it, three hours of fun and laughter between the two girls flew by. That summer, they spent so much time getting closer. When school started in the fall, they could only spend weekends together. Gabby had just gotten a new pet border collie named Joseph. He was black and white and loved to play with Gabby's large rubber bouncy ball. Cheyenne wanted a pet, too, but her parents didn't feel good about letting her have one. One night, Gabby called Mr. Keeney, asking to talk to him.

"Mr. Keeney, your daughter loves my new dog. I think you should consider letting her get one, too."

"I appreciate your concern, Gabby, but a pet is a big responsibility. After all, pets need to be fed, cleaned up after, and taken to the potty."

"Yes, sir, but I believe Cheyenne can do all of that. They also have this new cable, which you can attach outside your house, and all she has to do is click the dog chain onto the cable and then it can go by itself."

"You are very convincing, young lady. How about if you go along with us to the SPCA tomorrow to look?"

"Cool beans! What time can we go?"

"They are open until 6:00 p.m. We can pick you up about 4:30 after school. Will that work?"

"Great! My mom will come too. Can your wife Kelly come?"

"Of course. She will plan on coming also. We will bring our van in case we decide on a pet. And thank you for being such a good friend to our daughter."

"Oh, she's terrific! I'll see you then, Mr. Keeney!"

The next day at the SPCA, they couldn't find a pet that they liked. Cheyenne was very picky and she knew exactly what she wanted. Two days later, Phil found an article in their local newspaper about an animal shelter with pets in need of homes. The name of the shelter was "God's Wounded Creatures." It was called this because all the animals there had special needs. The Keeney's decided to go check it out, and when they got there, the manager named Margarete greeted them. Seeing that Cheyenne was blind, she thought of the first pet she would show the Keeney's. It was a little beagle named Faithful. His disability came about when a boy accidentally struck his voice box with his bicycle, causing him to lose the ability to bark.

"This is the dog I want. He has a special need like I do and needs someone who understands it just like my parents understand that I'm blind."

"Young lady, you bless me. So it is my honor to give this pet to you free of charge on one condition."

"Yes?" Cheyenne's voice became eager.

"I'd like you to check in with me on Faithful every three months."

"Thank you, ma'am, I will most definitely do that. This almost leaves me speechless like you, Faithful." They all chuckled. Next she asked her new dog, "Would you like to come home with me?" His tail began wagging rapidly back and forth.

"Look at that tail go! Young lady, I think you will have a friend for life." Margarete beamed.

Before they left, they signed all the proper papers and then happily waved good-bye to the staff. As soon as Cheyenne came home, she rushed to the phone and dialed Gabby's number. "You'll never guess what happened today!" she exclaimed.

"What's that?"

"I got a dog today and his name is Faithful. And he is very special."

"Oh? What makes him so special?" Gabby asked.

"He has a disability like I do. Only his disability is that he can't bark."

"You got a dog that can't bark? What a stupid idea."

Cheyenne was so angry that she just hung up the phone, and from then on she stopped visiting Gabby. Gabby soon realized the mistake she had made, but didn't know what to do. She told her parents what had happened and they tried to help by calling Cheyenne's parents, who then conveyed that Cheyenne's new dog was giving her more joy than the lost friendship had.

Six months passed and it was almost springtime. Gabby had become so depressed from losing her best friend that she even began paying less attention to her dog. The Keeney's still attended Gabby's church, but Gabby and Cheyenne still weren't talking to each other. One Sunday, the children's church pastor, Larry Gasteiger, came up with a plan to help them heal the relationship. He made an announcement to the whole congregation that day:

"Dear believers! I have come up with a new idea to reach our young people. We are having a dog owner's party at my house next Saturday. Bring your pet dog and swimming gear along. We will be having lunch at 12:30, and then a pet contest along with some swimming. I even have a special pool for the dogs. There will be a sign up sheet at the back of the church today."

Both girls complained. They didn't want to see each other, but their parents insisted that they go, suggesting they must both 'ruff-it-out.' Saturday came quickly and seven children came with their pet dogs. Barb with her boxer, Sharon with her shepard, George with his greyhound, Dave with his Dalmatian, Sally with her spitz, and Cheyenne and Gabby with their dogs. Pastor Larry and his wife Pat served hotdogs, baked beans, chips, pretzels, and many more party snacks. There were dog treats for the dogs, but no cats were allowed. While they all gathered around the table to eat, the boy next door spotted all the dogs. His name was Butch and he hated dogs. However, he did have two pet cats and they were both Siamese. They hated dogs, too. Butch waited until the group had all gathered for prayer and saw a window of opportunity. The biggest of the Siamese was named Goliath. Butch lifted him over the fence and let him go. What happened next was like watching the Daytona raceway. Joseph spotted Goliath first, and the rest followed after. Gabby screamed at the top of her lungs, "Joseph! Get back here!" to no avail. She and all the rest of the children took off running after their dogs and Pastor Larry picked up Cheyenne to join the chase.

"My flower bed!" screamed Mrs. Gasteiger as she saw it being pawed to the ground.

"Watch out for the clothes basket!" yelled the neighbor Mrs. Jones, who happened to be out doing laundry and noticed that she now had paw prints on her white blouses.

Mr. Wilson's farm was invaded next. There were lots of fruit trees and berry patches. The strawberry patch turned to strawberry juice, which would have been perfect for a strawberry float. Suddenly, the trip slowed to a stop as Goliath climbed to the top of a cherry tree. The first dog to arrive at the tree was the greyhound. He easily whipped up onto the tree's first branch to try to get the cat. Next was a rush of other dogs. The shepard reached up to a weaker branch and landed on top of Faithful. Just as he fell, Faithful's head hit a nearby rock that had been sticking out of the ground. In the midst of this commotion, Goliath leaped to the next cherry tree and snuck away. The shepard gave out a small whimper, distracting the other dogs. The owners arrived and were finally there to quiet their dogs. Soon enough, though, they all realized Cheyenne's dog wasn't moving and everything fell silent.

"We can go now. Everything is under control." Gabby quickly scooted toward Cheyenne, leading her away from the scene. "Pastor Larry is getting your dog for you so let's go back to his house," she coaxed. When they got back to the house, Gabby was surprised by what she heard next.

"You forget, Gabby, how good my hearing is. I know something happened at that tree that you didn't tell me."

"Oh? What was that?" Gabby said, pretending she didn't know.

"I know my dog can't bark. But I heard a thud when I got there and soon enough everything fell silent. Faithful died, didn't he?"

"Yes, Cheyenne. He hit his head on a rock and it killed him."

"Gabby, would you please take me back to my pet."

"Well, I know Pastor Larry was planning to bring your dog back for you." Just then the door swung open and Pastor Larry arrived with a blanket in his arms.

"Cheyenne, I have some sad news for you. I think this party was a bad idea today because now—"

"I know," Cheyenne interrupted, "Faithful is dead. Would you please give me my dog?"

"How did you know that, Cheyenne? Did Gabby tell you?"

"No, Pastor, I heard the thud and then it got quiet. That let me know something happened, and Faithful didn't come back to me."

"You have great discernment, young lady."

"I don't know what the word means, sir, but I do have good ears. Now where is Faithful?"

"He's here wrapped in this blanket. He has no outward bleeding, but I think it's all internal."

"Come here, Faithful. You're too good to leave me now. In Jesus' name, I speak life over you." Immediately, the blanket began to move. And a little head popped out and began licking her face. All those who were gathered around began gasping with eyes wide and jaws dropped. Faithful was alive again.

"Cheyenne, your faith has blessed me. Please forgive me for my actions these last few months," Gabby interjected with conviction.

"Forgive me, too, Gabby. God has a way to heal things that we can't. This time He chose to use a cat and some dogs."

"Children, today we've all learned a lesson. When God decides to do a miracle, He does it. And He'll use all that listen to Him," Pastor Gasteiger said. The children were all so touched by what happened that day, that they spread the news all over town. People were so touched by the story that families began coming to Cheyenne's church just to meet her and Faithful. By the end of that year, the church had even doubled in size. Gabby and Cheyenne's friendship became stronger than it had ever been before.

This is A.E. signing off and reminding you, boys and girls, that friendship is a powerful thing, and we must never take it for granted. Our verse for this story is Proverbs 18:24.

This chapter is dedicated to all those who can't see, but still have faith.

What A Way To Go

As the school year closed out, Gabby's and Cheyenne's families decided to take a trip to Ocean City, Maryland. School would let out on June 4 and the parents used the end of May to hammer out further details and set the trip date for June 11. This would give them a week to help the children pack and prepare with their families. Gabby was so excited that she couldn't stop talking about it. The morning of the trip, Gabby made sure she packed her favorite pair of bright pink rubber sandals with a seashell design.

"I'm ready to go, Mom and Dad. Is it time yet?" Gabby said with glee.

Christine and Bob also prepared for their last-minute needs. Christine was in charge of bringing the sunblock and Bob added his fishing rod to the mix. As soon as they arrived at the beach, Gabby and Cheyenne began picking up seashells.

"Isn't picking up seashells fun, Cheyenne?"

"Yes, Gabby. I can't see them, but they sure feel weird. The big one you told me to hold to my ear sounds like the sea is roaring."

"That's correct. It's because of the hollow part where a creature used to live. Aha, Cheyenne, my favorite find of today yet. It's a horseshoe crab!"

"A horseshoe crab? Does that mean it has shoes?" The puzzled look on Cheyenne's face included a slight frown.

"No, it's shaped like a horse's shoe, and it has another name, too. It can also be called a helmet crab."

"Oh, then that means it's wearing a helmet?"

"No, Cheyenne. Well, kind of. It's hard like a helmet. Here, feel it!" Just then, Gabby picked it up to hand to Cheyenne, and before she could get it to her friend, she jumped.

"YUCK!"

"What's wrong, Gabby?"

"EWW, I just picked up the crab and there were bugs all over it! It's dead!"

Just then, a new voice came from behind where they were playing. "What's cooking, girls?"

"Hi. Who are you?" Gabby insisted on knowing.

"I'm sorry if I startled you. My name is Charlie. And what are your names?"

"I am Gabby, and this is Cheyenne"

"Well it's nice to meet both of you. Are you sisters?"

"Not by blood, but definitely sisters in the Lord!" Gabby exclaimed.

"Oh, so you're both Christians then? Neeto! Me, too. Are you two from around here?"

"No, we're from Pennsylvania. How about you?"

"I live about five miles from here. I come to the beach almost every day."

"Doesn't that get boring after a while?"

"No. Hey, Cheyenne, what do you think about the horseshoe crab?" Charlie curiously looked over at her now.

"Well, I guess if Gabby says it's yucky, then it's yucky."

"Well, can't you make up your own mind by what you see?" he asked.

"No, because I can't see. I'm blind."

"Wow! That's kind of neat. Not that you're blind, but I can relate to you because I have cancer, and they've given me five months to live. I am writing letters to my friends to update them on how I'm doing. Can I add you to my list, Cheyenne, please?"

"Sure! My family can read them to me."

"Excuse me for interrupting, Charlie, but how long have you had cancer?" Gabby asked.

"About two years, but don't worry for me. I'm ready to meet Jesus, but I am really worried about my parents being sad."

A faraway look came into his eyes for a moment before Cheyenne added, "Speaking of your parents, where are they? I'd like to meet them."

"Yeah, my parents are up this way by the shore a bit. Follow me."

"Oh, our parents are up the same way. Let's go."

They all headed north on the beach about a thousand yards to where their parents were located. As they arrived, they noticed that all of their parents had already met. The families spent the rest of the day together getting acquainted. The next morning they all met at the sea shop as they had planned.

"Turtle rides!" Gabby read a sign in the window of the shop. "Mom, Dad can we please do that?"

"Sure, but they're not open now, honey. Have you ever done this, Charlie?" Christine asked.

"Of course. I even know the turtle's name. He's Oscar. You can even feed him at the end."

"That sounds like fun." Cheyenne smiled. "But let's go collect seashells while we are waiting for the shop to open."

They left for a few hours until it was time for the turtle rides. Oscar was a giant land turtle. Weighing over 300 pounds, he could easily transport each child thirty feet to the finish line. At the end, Gabby, Cheyenne, and Charlie fed him some lettuce leaves.

As soon as the rides had ended, they headed to the beach where they each took turns burying each other in the sand. The day ended with a walk on the beach with all of their families, and before waving good-bye, they made plans to meet at the sand sculpture for Sunday's service.

"This has been the most fun-filled day I've had in a long time," Gabby said as she looked at the setting sun and headed to the car.

"Amen to that! I can't wait to see Charlie again tomorrow!" Cheyenne beamed.

They attended the beach artist's church service where a man worked on a sand sculpture all weekend and then preach about it on Sunday morning. This weekend the artist made a sculpture of Jesus carrying his cross. The children went up to the man after the service and shared their story of how they met. He introduced them to his pastor who was there. He in turn asked the children if they could come to his church some Sunday and share their story. The parents all agreed to come the following Sunday.

"Wow, God is awesome! We make a new friend and God uses our friendship to share our testimony!" shouted Gabby.

"Yeah! A bold girl for Jesus, a blind believer, and a heaven-bound boy dying from cancer," Cheyenne added in.

"Wait till next week. It'll be an even greater feeling after we tell our story to a whole congregation!" Charlie exclaimed.

They all headed home after the service on the beach. During the following week, Gabby and Cheyenne discussed their new friendship and how they would tell their story. Charlie got their phone numbers and called them before Sunday. Both Gabby's dad and Cheyenne's dad got the address of the church and discussed who would drive. Phil agreed to use his van since it was bigger and he had just gotten a new GPS. Throughout the week, many discussions occurred to hammer out the details.

Soon enough, Sunday morning came. They all packed into the van and headed to Maryland. The name of the church was "The Rock," and they arrived thirty minutes early. Charlie's parents were already there. The pastor knew his parents since they had been at this church a few times before. It was a large church with more than two thousand attendants every Sunday morning. The main service began at 10:30 a.m. and ended at noon. The children were to share from 11:00-11:15 a.m. Just before it was their time to talk, the pastor gave a brief introduction.

"Dear Saints! Today we have three special guests to share a true story of pure friendship. Their names are Gabby Boral, Cheyenne Keeney, and our own local prize, a patient who's fighting cancer, Charlie Snell. Please give them a warm welcome and a round of applause as they come to share."

The congregation began clapping and then took their seats.

"Hello. I am Gabby Boral. I am a girl from central Pennsylvania and I believe that friendship builds character in people. My best friend here is Cheyenne Keeney. She's a blind girl that once laid her hands and prayed over her dead dog and it lived again. Please welcome her as she comes to share her part of our story."

The audience gave another round of applause before Cheyenne began.

"Hi! I am Cheyenne Keeney and I live near Gabby. I lost my eyesight as a toddler. Mom was cleaning the bathroom and I knocked over the bucket of cleaning chemicals that went in my eyes and blinded me. This past year, Gabby and I became friends. We lost our friendship for a while, and then God brought us back together using some dogs and a cat at our youth pastor's house back in the fall. God is always doing miracles when we're together. Last week, we made a new friend from picking up a stinky, bug-filled horseshoe crab on the beach. Our friend Charlie is now going to tell you his part of the story."

"Hi! It's little old me. Charlie Snell. I'm a devil-defeating, bible-thumping, and cancer-fighting believer. My new friends here have come from me being nosey as usual. Friends usually come along when you're trying to reach out to new people. I reached out to them while observing a horseshoe crab. He was wearing his helmet. Are you wearing yours today? That's right! I'm talking about the helmet of salvation. Are you saved from hell? Or are you still wearing your shell of flesh? Jesus loves you."

Hearing these words caused a wave of emotion to fall over the audience. In silence, the pastor, moved by this anointing, stood up and put his arm around Charlie's shoulder. "Son, you just stole my sermon." He turned from Charlie to the congregation saying, "God is here today to bring salvation free to you so you can become his friend. If you would like to know the Jesus whom these children have shared, come forward at this time to meet him."

"Pastor?"

"Yes, what is it, Gabby?" He looked at her with a peaceful expression on his face.

"God wants to heal friendships here today, too. Can we extend the call for healing between friends as well?"

"Most certainly we will. If you are here today and you need a healing over a broken relationship or friendship, please come forward at this time."

Within the next few minutes, the altar was packed with more than 100 people. Tears were falling from faces, people were embracing, and smiles were glowing all over the room. The pastor turned to the choir and asked them to sing a song. They began to sing "What a Friend We Have in Jesus" and at the end of the service the orchestra played the song "And Friends Are Friends Forever."

News of the healing during that service spread and within the next two months the children were asked to speak at three more churches. Over 300 lives were changed by the power of God and 500 relationships were restored.

Three months passed. Charlie's parents contacted the Keeneys and Borals to let them know that Charlie was near death. They all took a trip that weekend to visit him. He was so sick he couldn't even get out of bed, but when Gabby and Cheyenne entered his room, he sat up for the first time in two days.

A few laughs were shared remembering the last few months. Charlie shared with them that he had had a dream that they'd all be together someday and Jesus would enter the room.

"Look! There he is!" Charlie's face turned even paler, and he pointed and waved toward the end of the room. "Hi, Jesus!" A smile came to his face just before Charlie fell back into his bed and died. Everyone cried, but they could feel the presence of God in the room.

"What a way to go to heaven. Saying hi to Jesus, and then leave!" Gabby announced as tears welled up and flowed down her cheeks.

"Amen! Son, be at peace. We will all miss you but we will see you again someday," Charlie's dad said as he held his son.

Charlie's burial service the following week was very special. Several people stood up and shared testimony of how Charlie had touched their lives. Cheyenne and Gabby were given the honor of laying the final flowers on his casket before he was buried. In the months to come, the girls missed their friend greatly. They took the opportunity to speak in two more churches and blessed more people.

One weekend, Gabby wanted to visit Charlie's grave. Her parents agreed that it would be a good step to heal the loss of her friend. Cheyenne couldn't go since she had other plans, but she sent along one of her stuffed teddy bears to give to Charlie's little sister and she named it Charles. When they arrived at the graveyard, Gabby put flowers on the grave. They were lilacs, Charlie's favorite.

"Charlie, I miss you buddy. I hope they have a horseshoe crab up there to remember us by. We've had more chances to tell people about our great friendship and I know that God is still using our story today." Just then, Gabby noticed another family gathered at another grave across the field. Jesus put it in her heart to go introduce herself to them.

"Hi. I'm Gabby. Who are you visiting here today?"

"Hello, this is our son's grave. His name is Eric. He died three months ago from cancer," answered a pale-faced woman with dark hair. "Why, God, did you take my son from me?" Her tone changed from defeated to enraged.

"Lady, I understand your pain."

"No, you don't. It should have been me!" Tears left her tormented blue eyes.

"Lady, God didn't take your son. Cancer took you son. God did a healing for your son by taking him home."

"Boy, you're a bold young lady to speak to a stranger like that." The middle-aged woman wiped some tears from her face.

"No, just a fool for Jesus. He loves you and died for you. Do you know him?"

"I know who he is. Yes, of course."

"Then just accept his gift of salvation and fall in love with him, and he will heal you of your loss," Gabby said assuredly. "John 10:10 says that a thief steals, kills, and destroys, but Jesus came to give us life to the fullest amount."

The woman and her family were so amazed at Gabby's words that they wanted to hear more. So Gabby then shared about her friends Cheyenne and Charlie. They were all so touched by Gabby's wisdom that they introduced themselves and thanked her.

"You bring tears to my eyes. You have a way of peace about you," the mother said.

"That's Jesus. He is the prince of peace."

"We need that peace."

"Good! Let's pray to get that peace."

Gabby then led the whole family to the Lord in that graveyard and they become friends. When Gabby got home she called Cheyenne and told her what had happened and they rejoiced together. They were becoming a soul-winning operation for Jesus.

After a week went by, Gabby received some shocking news. Her dad needed to change jobs and move 200 miles from home. It was possible that they might all have to move. Pastor Elmer wanted to recognize the girls together in case this move happened, so he held a special service to recognize all that God was doing through them. Each girl received a trophy that said "To God's little soul winner. Don't quit!" Gabby then gave a little speech before the congregants:

"To my church family. If I do leave, you will go with me in spirit. Cheyenne will always be a part of my heart, and God is awesome!"

Gabby said her thank yous and stepped down.

Dear reader,
Remember that friendship is a special gift. Never take it lightly, and always embrace it with truth and respect. If you don't know Jesus as your Savior, please write or call our ministry today. We want you to be a part of God's family, too.
~A.E.

This chapter is dedicated to all the cancer patients around the world. You are invited to read John 15:13.

☺

C.T.W. Ministries
671 Maryland Ave
York, Pa 17403
717-659-8496

The Rabbit

THE FOLLOWING WEEK, BOB RECEIVED a notice that the new position would be temporary. He would be at the other plant for just three months due to someone being on maternity leave. He took the job since it was an extra $300 a week. His family would stay at home and he would stay with relatives while he worked. On weekends he would visit Christine and Gabby.

"Gabby, I will be away during the week and you will have to help your mom around here. I'm giving you the following chores to do. You'll be in charge of the trash, the garden, and feeding your pets."

"Okay, Dad. I will do that. Will you be checking in?"

"I will be calling every day. Please keep your room clean, too. Your mother will have enough to do with her regular duties, plus fix-ups and mowing the lawn."

"Please say hi to Uncle Sam and Aunt Mary for us. And enjoy the farm and your new job." Gabby smiled with a look of adventure in her eyes.

"I will, and if you do a good job, we will take a trip when I get back after the three months."

"Great! To Disney?"

"I'm not sure where we will go until I see how well you've done."

"Well, don't worry, Dad. I will do a great job!" Gabby twinkled and gave herself an inner vote of confidence.

That week, Bob prepared for his move while a new family was moving in across the street. It was a family from Idaho named Matson. Even though Gabby was learning her new chores, she found time to meet her new neighbors. It was a family of four with one boy, one girl, and their parents.

"Hello! I am Gabby Boral from across the street. Welcome to our neighborhood."

"Nice to meet you, Gabby. We are the Matson family. This is my daughter Shaneen, my son Ricky, my wife Carletta, and my name is Gene."

"Why did you guys decide to move here?" Gabby curiously inquired.

"My company in Idaho closed up and this was the only place that had an opening in my profession."

"What do you do, Mr. Matson?" Gabby asked, even more inquisitively this time.

"My job is kind of difficult to describe. Let's just say that I help people in trouble."

"Sounds unusual. Are you a cop or something like that?"

"Not really. However, I do talk with policemen a lot."

"Well, that's neat. I would like it if Shaneen could come over to play once you get settled in."

"Sure! By the end of the week you are welcome to come over Gabby," Carletta said with a welcoming smile.

"Our little farm has a lot of land and you could play in the fields," Gene added.

"Gabby, do you have any pets?" Shaneen's bright eyes looked excited as she asked.

"Why, yes! I have a pet dog name Joseph, and a fish tank full of guppies and mollies."

"Well, I have a pet rabbit named Ollie. I keep him in a cage outside. He's pretty young still. I got him from a friend back in Idaho as a going away present and my dad bought me a new cage just before we left."

"Where are you going to put him?" Gabby wondered.

"In the wooden shack out in the backyard next to the small barn."

"Oh neat! Well, I know you have a lot to do here so I'll catch you all later."

"Yeah, we have the whole moving van to empty before it gets dark. I'll talk to you later." Shaneen smiled and waved.

Gabby waved back to the family and headed home to complete her chores. By Thursday night, the Matsons were all settled in and things were where they wanted them to be. Bob was all packed up for his trip to Stroudsburg, Pennsylvania.

"Daddy, what will you do on the farm when you get home from work each day?" Gabby asked.

"Well, that will be up to Uncle Sam and Aunt Mary, but probably feed the chickens and clean the milk machines."

"Yeah, and probably eat some of Aunt Mary's famous pies! Yum-yum!"

"And, of course, some of Grandma Katie's sugar cookies, too."

"Be careful with Grandma's superstitious ways. And don't break any mirrors or glass or she'll stay away from you."

"No worries, daughter. Enjoy the new neighbors. I met them all yesterday and they seem very nice. And by the way they're calling for bad storms this weekend so be safe."

"If it gets real bad, Dad, can I bring Joseph in the house?"

"Yes, but make sure you take him out regularly. He's not housebroken. And also, give some veggies from our greenhouse to our new neighbors as a welcome gift."

"Okay, Dad. Are you leaving in the morning?"

"Yes, I'll be leaving early to beat the traffic on the interstate. Route 33 can get very busy. I will call when I arrive, but I'll be stopping at the power plant before I get to the farm."

"Bob, I have your bags ready for you. And don't forget your shaver in the morning," Christine said.

"Yes, dear, and if anything happens, please give me a call. You know Aunt Mary has strict bedtime rules, and her favorite saying is 'Early to bed, early to rise, makes one healthy, wealthy, and wise.' Bedtime is at eight o'clock, and you're up before dawn. Breakfast is at 5:00 a.m."

"Wow! That's even before the chickens get up!" Gabby's eyes got a bit wider.

"Yes! The rooster usually crows at 5:00 a.m."

Friday morning came and Bob left. Gabby had plans to visit Shaneen's farm that day. They had five acres of land and four were used for planting crops. Mr. Matson was planting some tomatoes and squash that morning.

"Hi, Mr. Matson. Planting some veggies I see. I just brought you a bag of some from our greenhouse."

"Thank you. That's very thoughtful. Shaneen is in the shed with her rabbit. You can go see her."

"Thanks. I'll see you later."

"Hi, Gabby. This is Ollie that I told you about. He's about three months old and is what they call a jackrabbit."

"Oh! Then he has two names. Ollie and Jack."

"Ha ha. No, a jackrabbit is the type of rabbit he is. He can run very fast."

"Well, be careful not to let him loose or he'll get away."

"I'm taking him inside right now to feed him some warm milk. I have a large box inside to keep him in."

As they entered the house, Mrs. Matson was baking a fresh batch of chocolate chip cookies. She also mixed up some orange flavored Kool-Aid.

"Hello, Gabby. Welcome to our home. Shaneen, here is your bottle for the rabbit. And remember to feed him over the tub in case you spill."

"Yes, Mother. Where's my brother?"

"He left to go play basketball at the school with some of the neighbor boys. He will be back by lunch."

They took Ollie to the bathroom and fed him his bottle. Then Shaneen gave Gabby the house tour. It had five bedrooms, two bathrooms, a living room, kitchen, dining room, and a full basement. There was a small attic, and a balcony outside of the master bedroom.

The morning passed by quickly and lunchtime came. Gabby was permitted to stay until three thirty that day. She was excited for lunch, which turned out to be a feast.

They had mac and cheese with stewed tomatoes, pot roast, and for desert a chocolate cheesecake covered with whipped cream.

"What a nice meal, Mrs. Matson. Thank you so much. Did you make the cheesecake?"

"No. That came from Weis Markets. By the way girls, the weather is going to get bad real soon. They just announced on the radio that a band of storms is headed this way. Please stay inside after lunch.

"How about Ollie, Mom?"

"He should go out in his large pen out back so he has more space to run around. He might get too excited in here and break his box."

"Okay, Mom. I'll take him out right away."

"Yes, but it's already getting dark outside so hurry up."

"I'll go along with you, Shaneen," Gabby stated.

They got up from the table and grabbed Ollie as they went out the back door. Suddenly, there was a flash of lightning and Ollie jumped from Shaneen's arms and took off.

"Ollie! Come back here!" Shaneen yelled. But he was quickly out of sight.

"Girls! Get in here. The storm's getting worse!" Carletta yelled from the porch.

Gabby yelled for Shaneen but she was running to find Ollie. She headed inside, and looking at Mrs.

Matson, said, "Let's pray now!" Mrs. Matson wasn't a Christian, but she accepted Gabby's idea.

"Dear Jesus, please keep Ollie and Shaneen safe during this storm. Protect them with your mighty hand and surround them with your angels. Amen!"

"That was nice, Gabby. Thank you," Carletta said. "I'm going to get my rain gear and go find her."

"Mrs. Matson, don't worry. We prayed. God will protect them both. Just wait for the storm to quiet down a little."

About twenty minutes later the storm was calming down. The lightning had stopped and it was drizzling just a little. Then Mrs. Matson, Ricky, and Gabby went outside to look for Shaneen and Ollie. Ricky went to the right, Gabby checked out the barn and the shed, and Carletta looked across the field.

"Over here!" hollered Ricky.

They all met near a stack of straw outside the barn. There they found Ollie lying on top of some straw with a piece of Shaneen's clothing under him. At the same time Mr. Matson pulled into the driveway.

"What's going on here?" he asked when he got to the group.

"Dad! We're looking for Shaneen. She went out during the storm and we don't know where she is. But we just found Ollie lying here on a piece of her clothes in this pile of straw."

"Well then, let's start digging. Ricky, you take the right side, I'll take the middle, and Mom can take the left. Gabby, you can hold Ollie."

They began to rip through the large pile of straw that the prior owners had left behind. Suddenly, they heard a voice say, "What are you all looking for?"

"Shaneen," her mother gasped, "where did you come from?"

"I just crawled out of that big plastic barrel in the barn. That's where I hid during the storm."

"But how did this piece of clothing get here?" Ricky asked.

"In my rush toward the barn, I got caught on a nail and my skirt ripped. I guess the wind blew it here."

"Well, that's one smart rabbit." Gene Matson began to smile. "Ollie knew it belonged to you. So he laid on it to feel close to you."

"Ollie, you're such a good boy! Thank you for saving my piece of clothing."

"Daughter, I thought we lost you, but Gabby prayed and we're all safe." Carletta beamed joyously.

"Mom, can we go to her church this Sunday? I like her faith and I want to learn more about it."

"Me, too!" Ricky added. "One of the boys at the basketball game today told me that Jesus loves me. Nobody ever said anything like that to me before. I know he is real after today."

"That sounds wonderful! What do you think, Gene?" Carletta turned to her husband.

"Sounds like a great plan!" he agreed.

They headed inside and Carletta made hot chocolate. Once they were settled in, Shaneen commented, "We're going to need directions to your church for Sunday morning."

"Oh no, you won't. I'll call our bus driver and have him pick you all up at your house."

"Wow, a bus for church and an escort? That's what I call service. What time should we be ready?"

"The bus arrives at 9:15 a.m. and church begins at ten. Oh my, look at the time. It's almost 3:30! I need to get home. I bet Mom is worried." Gabby said her good-byes and thank yous to the Matsons.

"Thanks, Gabby, for your prayers. Boy, that barrel sure felt safe during the storm."

"Hey, sis! This was a real hare-raising experience, huh?" Ricky asked from across the room and chuckled.

"Ha ha, Ricky, very funny. Maybe we should go to the local gift shop and buy you a rabbit's foot in remembrance of today!"

That Sunday morning, everyone in the Matson family accepted Jesus as their savior. They also began attending Gabby's church regularly.

Boys and girls, when you're going through a storm, remember God is with you. Today's scripture is from Psalm 23:4. Remember what God can do in the midst of the storm. This is A.E. signing off.

This chapter is dedicated to the Matson family.

Made in the USA
Middletown, DE
22 July 2017